Calculation

Calculation

by
Steven P. Marini

Gypsy Shadow Publishing

Calculation
by
Steven P. Marini

All rights reserved
Copyright © February 26, 2014, Steven P. Marini
Cover Art Copyright © 2014, Charlotte Holley

Gypsy Shadow Publishing, LLC.
Lockhart, TX
www.gypsyshadow.com

Names, characters and incidents depicted in this book are products of the author's imagination, or are used fictitiously. Any resemblance to actual events, locales, organizations, or persons, living or dead, is entirely coincidental and beyond the intent of the author or the publisher.

No part of this book may be reproduced or shared by any electronic or mechanical means, including but not limited to printing, file sharing, and email, without prior written permission from Gypsy Shadow Publishing, LLC.

Library of Congress Control Number: 2014940188

eBook ISBN: 978-1-61950-200-0
Print ISBN: 978-1-61950-201-7

Published in the United States of America

First eBook Edition: May 1, 2014
First Print Edition: May 8, 2014

Other novels by Steven P. Marini:

Connections
A Jack Contino Crime Story

This vigorous, well-plotted crime concoction takes a straight-on look at the tangles and snares involved in stepping outside the "social contract," and it's a kind of morality tale without the classroom lecture. It's pretty well done, too. The author has wisely limited his word count, so it feels just about right, and we're left with the sense of an inaugural job well done.

—The Barnstable Patriot

Aberration
A Jack Contino Crime Story

Author Marini again shows his mettle when it comes to creating a great storyline . . ."

—The Barnstable Patriot

Aberration takes off like a bullet with a cool hero: Jack Contino, a cop's cop, who knows a thing or two about criminals, breaking cases and chasing down a cold one. You'll find yourself rooting for him all the way. And if it's the late 1970s you're nostalgic for, you'll feel right at home with this nifty mystery.

—Jordan Rich
Chart Productions, Inc.
WBZ Radio

Dedication

To my special gal, Louise, without whom I would not have been able to finish this book.

Chapter One

I hate these damn, freakin' places, condos, condos, condos. The Cape is supposed to have quaint little cottages in quaint little villages, here and there. La,la,la. Saw the wife and kiddie leave, so now it's just you and me, booze man.

I'd seen death like this before. Thirty plus years of police work in Boston gave me plenty of experience. Now I was with the police department in Dennis, Massachusetts, on Cape Cod, the place Patti Page sang about, *Old Cape Cod*, quaint and quiet, with salt air everywhere. It was the late 1970s and I was still a cop, only now I was trying to take it slow and ease my way into retirement soon. This had all the markings of a Mob hit. They don't get creative. When the Mob wants to execute somebody, they don't have time to make a ceremony out of it. They usually have someone the victim trusts and lets the killer get close. Then, the killer turns the tables on the target, the ultimate betrayal of trust. This one fit the profile.

The guy took a single bullet to the back of the head in his West Dennis townhouse, shattering the peaceful October Sunday afternoon he was enjoying while his wife and small daughter were out. His body lay on the kitchen floor by the counter. It was a small kitchen, with yellow appliances against a light green wall. A guy could stand at the range and spin around to be at the sink. There was a bottle of Scotch and two glasses with ice on the counter near him, spoiled by blood spatter.

I got the call while off duty at home with my wife, Natalie. We were cleaning house when Sergeant Jim Pearson called me. My home is in West Yarmouth, so it took me about fifteen minutes to get to the scene. I looked around the kitchen and surrounding area with Jim while the forensic techs did their thing. Pearson was my right hand on the Dennis PD, a smart twenty-year man. He was about

Calculation Steven P. Marini

six foot-two and built like a linebacker, a good man to have beside you if things got rough.

"What have you got on him, Jim?"

"He's Robert Schroeder, thirty-three years old, owner of West Dennis Liquors on Main Street. I've been in there myself and chatted with him a little. He's owned the store outright for a couple of years, after buying out his partner. That's what he told me once. His wife was out when it happened. She and her little girl came home and found him. Fortunately, she was able to block her daughter from seeing this. She's with a neighbor next door. Mom is in the master bedroom with Officer Karen Orlando."

"Speaking of neighbors . . ."

"Some officers are questioning people now," said Pearson.

"Good. I'll talk to the wife, if she's up to it."

"She's okay with that, Jack. I spoke to her briefly and told her she'd have to talk to you, too."

"Fine. While I see her, check on the officers canvassing the neighbors."

"Got it."

Anne Schroeder was sitting on the bed when I came in. She held a handkerchief to help her wipe back tears. I asked Officer Orlando to remain.

"Hello, Mrs. Schroeder, I'm Detective Jack Contino. I'm in charge of the investigation."

She looked to be in her early thirties, a very good looking woman, and was well composed, considering what had just happened. She seemed small and frail, but when she spoke, there was strength in her surprisingly deep voice.

"Yes, Detective, Sergeant Pearson said you'd need to talk to me. I understand. I want to help any way I can to catch whoever did this."

"I'm very sorry for your loss, Mrs. Schroeder. I know this must be very hard for you, but I need to get as much information as I can quickly. If, however, you need some time, I understand."

"No. That's okay, Detective. Go ahead."

I don't know how people in her situation can do it. Somehow they pull it together, for a while, anyway.

"Did your husband have any enemies that you know of?"

Mrs. Schroeder took a breath and paused a moment before speaking. She looked at me, then diverted her eyes, gazing toward the window across the large bedroom. The room was nicely decorated with a king size bed and matching cherry wood dressers, all new. The tan wall-to-wall carpet felt like a cushion under my big feet.

"Detective, my husband had a partner when they bought the liquor store five years ago. He was an old high school friend of Bob's. Bob worked very hard to make his business a success, since it was always his dream to own his own business. Well, George, that's his friend, George Brady, didn't have the same energy for work and they didn't see eye to eye about how to grow the business. Bob wanted to open another store after a few years, but George didn't want to do that. He just wanted to enjoy the profits from the current store and live like he was on a permanent vacation. I guess you could say they had a falling out."

"Did it ever get violent?"

"No, but they had some real shouting matches. I thought once that they were going to fight, but George slammed his fist against a wall at the store and walked out. The only solution was to buy George out, which Bob did two years ago. It meant selling the ranch house we had to get the money, but as soon as we sold it, Bob did the buyout. It drained our savings almost to nothing, but it was the only way. It was worth it, though. Bob hired an assistant to help him and a couple of part timers. I work there, too, part time when Janie, that's our daughter, is in school. It's been paying off and we moved into this condo unit seven months ago."

"Who was working the store today, the assistant?"

"Yes. My God, he doesn't know what's happened. I didn't think to call him. I'd better do that now."

"Relax, Mrs. Schroeder, I'll have some officers go over there and tell him to close up. Does he lock up the cash in a safe?"

"Yes. There's one in the back room."

"We'll have him do that and tell him you'll have to close the store for a while."

"Thank you, Detective."

She gave me the name of the assistant and I passed that on to Pearson, who sent an officer to the store.

"Mrs. Schroeder, do you have George Brady's address and phone number?"

"I have that information in our address book, but I don't know if he still lives there. He was in Harwich."

She started to get up, but I suggested that I could get that information in a minute. I wanted to keep her talking.

"Did Mr. Schroeder ever have any other business dealings with people who he didn't see eye to eye with?"

"No. He got along fine with the owner of the building and everyone else I know of."

"I'd like to get the building owner's name and information, too. Did your husband have any hobbies or activities that might have involved large sums of money?"

"You mean, like gambling, Detective? It's a fair question. I'm not offended that you asked. No, he didn't gamble. His whole life was his family and the store."

I didn't mean to insult her and was relieved by her response. "Of course, Mrs. Schroeder. I didn't mean to imply anything." I took a breath. "Is there anything else that you can tell me? Is there anybody else who might have a grudge of some sort against your husband?"

She shook her head, holding it high as she spoke, despite the tears.

"No, Detective. Bob was a fine man. He was kind and gracious to everyone."

"Okay, Mrs. Schroeder, you understand that you can't stay here now. We have to secure the crime scene, probably for a few days. Is there anyone you can stay with? If not, we'll take you and your daughter to a motel at the town's expense."

"My sister lives in Sandwich. I've already called her, and she's on her way."

"Fine. Pack some things. Officer Orlando will help you. Your sister won't be able to enter, so we'll let you know when she arrives."

"That's all right, Detective."

She eased her petite body off the bed and walked over to a closet and started collecting clothes. She wore tan Capri pants and a pale blue T-shirt. With white tennis shoes, she seemed to float across the floor. She turned back toward me and I saw her beautiful blue eyes, now tinged with sadness.

"Our luggage is in the basement storage area. May I get it?"

"Of course," I said. "Officer Orlando will help with that, as I said. Tell her whatever you need. Thank you, Mrs. Schroeder. I know this is very difficult for you. You've been most helpful."

I collected the contact information for George Brady and Henry Santino, the owner of the building that contained West Dennis liquors. It was very early in the investigation, but the only lead we had so far was Brady. I hoped this would be an open-and-shut case, but they rarely are.

I went back into the kitchen to look at the body and surrounding area again. The Medical Examiner was still there. "Looks like someone he knew came over and the victim was fixing some drinks for them, then, pop, a single bullet to the back of the head."

"An easy call for you on cause of death," I said. "I hope it will be just as easy to find his killer, but I doubt it. The blood spatter ruined a good single malt, Glen Fiddich. What a nice quiet Cape Cod town I moved into."

The M.E. snickered as he finished up. He knew my situation.

I had made a career in law enforcement in Boston as part of the Metropolitan District Commission Police Department, aka the METs. I took a bullet in the gut a couple of years ago while nailing a Mob hit man named Ben Secani. I was in my early fifties at the time and my wife, Natalie, decided that she'd had enough with my cops-and-robbers career in Boston. She wanted to move away from greater Boston and live a peaceful life somewhere.

Two years after that shooting, I heard about an opening on the Dennis Police Department on Cape Cod. I was going to apply for the job. Nat preferred that I go into another line of work altogether, but I just wasn't ready. There are too many bad guys out there, one in particular named Tommy Shea, who ran a Mob gang out of Somerville, my old home town. We knew each other for a long time and even had a joust outside a bar in my early years on the METs. He cut me with a piece of glass from a beer bottle before I slapped him silly. The scar didn't show too badly now.

The chance to draw a pension and get a full-time salary for a few years meant I could make sure Nat had enough assets if something happened to me. Or, better yet, we'd just pile up a hefty nest egg for our very late years.

My former partner and longtime buddy, Leo Barbado, was still helping me keep a sharp eye out for Tommy Shea and company. About a year ago, Shea's buddy Sal DiFino, aka Sammy White, put out a contract on me. We got to DiFino first and put him away for a long time, since we also got him for multiple counts of extortion, assault and battery, loan sharking, and conspiracy to commit murder. But Shea was well-insulated and stayed free to run his club of hoods. He and/or DiFino might have killed a female FBI agent who did undercover work, but got too close with DiFino. She went missing just as we were closing in on Sal. Shea was always on my radar, always would be until one of us was done.

I walked out of the kitchen, through the living room and out the front door. Jim Pearson was returning from checking on the other officers' progress and he met me on the sidewalk that led from the parking area.

"Any luck?" I asked.

"Nope. None of the residents saw anything or anybody suspicious. It was all very quiet today. No unusual noises, either, like a gunshot."

"Could've used a silencer?"

"Could have. That would make sense," said Jim. "What did you get out of Mrs. Schroeder?"

"She said her husband had a falling-out with his business partner and bought him out a couple of years ago. The business has been doing well and they moved in here seven months ago. Prosperity can breed jealousy in ex-partners and that can be a motive for murder for some people. I got his name and an address, so I'll pay him a visit. Want to come along?"

"I wouldn't miss it, Jack. I'll ride with you."

"My car awaits."

The ride to Harwich, the next town east of Dennis, took us to a duplex, single story on Bank Street. I parked on the curb in front of the house. There was a brown Dodge Dart in the driveway. Jim went around back and I approached the front door for the unit to the left, number fifteen.

I knocked hard before I noticed the doorbell. I rang that, too. In a few seconds, a tall blonde woman in jeans

and a blue T-shirt answered. I guessed her to be in her mid-thirties, a good looker, but showing some dark under the eyes.

"Hello," I said. "I'm Detective Contino from the Dennis Police. I'm looking for George Brady. Is he here?"

"Yeah, he's here."

She paused to look me up and down and her face didn't show approval. "What's the trouble, Detective?"

"I'd like to speak with Mr. Brady, please."

She gave me a sneer and walked back into the house. "George, there's a cop here to see you. Have you been a bad boy?"

"Very funny," said a voice. A man, near six feet tall, broad shouldered and sporting a healthy gut, appeared from the next room and walked toward me at the door. He was wearing khaki pants and a wrinkled white shirt with the sleeves rolled up at the elbows. His brown loafers clanked against the wooden floor in the hallway. He looked like a guy who couldn't stay in shape and didn't try too hard at it.

"What can I do for you?"

"Are you George Brady?"

"Yes sir, in the flesh. What's up?"

"May I come in? There's something I need to talk to you about."

"Sure. Sure. Come on in."

We moved into the living room, dimmed by drawn curtains, and took seats opposite each other. He made himself comfortable, sitting back in the middle of a cheaply made sofa, the kind with wooden arm rests, that was at a right angle to the end wall where a large TV perched on a flimsy stand. I settled into an excuse for an easy chair opposite him. His girlfriend walked away and into the kitchen without speaking.

"I'm Detective Contino, Dennis PD. I'd like to know if you've been over to your old partner's house today."

Brady's eyes widened.

"You mean Bob Schroeder? Why do you want to know that?"

"He was murdered this afternoon, probably between noon and two o'clock."

"Murdered? Holy shit, man. Really?" He leaned forward, his mouth hanging open.

"Yeah, really. He took a gunshot to the back of the head at close range, while he was pouring two Scotches in his kitchen, like the killer was someone he knew well enough to offer him a drink."

"Oh, wait there a minute, Detective. You don't think I did it, do you?"

"Did you?"

"No, of course not. I've been here with Tina all day. Hey look, we broke up our partnership a couple of years ago. I haven't spoken to him since."

"But you two go way back, I understand. You were friends in school."

"Yeah, that's right. We were buds all through high school and stayed close through college, even though we went to different schools. He married Anne and I stayed single, more fun that way, as I see it. Anyway, we put our money together and opened the liquor store after waiting a few years when the business became available. We figured it was a gold mine and it was."

"Then why did you sell out?"

"It was doing great but Bob wanted to expand it, you know, open up another store. I figured why mess with success. Leave things as they were and live happily ever after. But he couldn't leave well enough alone. He even drew out another license application without consulting me. We almost had it out over that. So I said you buy me out and you can do whatever you want with the damned store. We eventually agreed on a price, though that wasn't easy either."

His story matched the picture I had of him from Mrs. Schroeder. He was an unambitious slob.

"The buyout must have set you up pretty good."

"It was good, but not enough to live on the rest of my life. I tried a couple of things that didn't go so well, so now I'm selling cars in Hyannis and doing all right. I bought this place and rent out the other side to cover the mortgage, almost."

Brady talked fast and I had to stop him short to get a word in. Car salesman. It figures. Guys like this are typical, selling high-ticket items.

"Do you own a gun, Mr. Brady?"

"Yes, as a matter of fact, I do. I keep it for protection. I used to have it at the store. It's registered properly and I'm licensed to carry. I can show you the paper work."

"Good. I'll need to see that and the gun. Now would be good."

The blonde woman came running into the living room. "Hey, there's a cop out back. What's he doing? I suppose he's with you."

I was getting used to her sneer. "Yes, he's with me. Miss, would you mind telling him to come in here?"

"Yeah, I'd mind. Tell him yourself."

What a snotty little brat. I looked at her without speaking, then switched to Brady and said to stay in the living room while I called Jim. I went into the kitchen, glancing back to see if Brady did as I said, opened the back door and motioned for Jim to join us inside. The sink was full of dirty dishes and the room smelled of stale beer. I went back to the living room without waiting for Pearson.

When Jim reached us, I told Brady to show me the gun and his papers. I followed him into the bedroom to be on the safe side. This guy might be a killer.

"What's the matter, Detective? Don't you trust me?"

"Just following procedure, Mr. Brady. That's all."

The queen size bed looked too small for Brady and his girlfriend, and the old hardwood floor had scratches in it. Two of the walls each had a small window which didn't let in enough light. There were non-matching night stands on each side of the bed. Brady opened a drawer to one of them and started to reach inside. "Hold it," I said. "Grab it by the barrel."

Brady did as I commanded, lifting up a .22 caliber Smith and Wesson hand gun. "Let me see it," I said, and he handed it to me handle first. It was not what I was expecting.

"This is a .22 caliber, not the best choice for personal protection."

"Maybe not, but it will do fine if I have to shoot a thief in the head. And the price is more to my liking than a .357 cannon."

I looked at the barrel. There were no marks of any kind, like threading from a silencer. I doubted that this was a murder weapon. The paperwork was in order, so I gave the gun back to Brady and he closed the drawer with the gun back inside. We returned to the living room.

"Miss, I'll need your full name and address, please."

"I wondered when you'd get around to that. I'm Christine Johnson, Tina to my friends. You can call me Miss Johnson, and I live here."

I made a mental note. "So you were here all day with George?"

"Correct."

Brady scratched the back of his neck. "Look, Detective, I had a breakup with Schroeder, but I still thought of him as a friend, even if we didn't keep in touch. I didn't kill him. I could never do that."

"Can you think of anyone who could?"

"No, not like this. I mean, I always felt we were at risk in a liquor store, you know, from street punks. That's why I got the gun. But I can't think of anyone who was close to Bob who could go into his home and kill him. That's incredible."

Brady's faced was flushed. Reality was hitting him.

"Well, that'll be all for now, Mr. Brady." I gave him my card and gave him the usual stuff about calling me if he thought of anything helpful. I didn't expect much from him. Jim and I got back in my car.

"He's not the killer," I said. "He's got a .22 Smith and Wesson, clean and cold. I doubt he's ever so much as fired it at a range. Ballistics will confirm my suspicions, but I don't think a .22 made that crater in Schroeder's head. Brady's not the type. He's a talker and a slider, not a tough guy. His girlfriend's got a lot of attitude. What a piece of work."

"Maybe she did it for him, using another gun. Maybe the .22 is just a decoy," said Jim as we drove back to the station.

"Not likely, Jimbo. Remember, there were two glasses of Scotch, not three. They'd both have to have been there, since their alibi is that they were both here all day, covering for each other. So we have to find some evidence that a couple was there, man and woman, not a single visitor and we have to find another gun. You're stretching, Jim."

"Yes, I guess so. I'm just searching for possibilities."

"That's all right. We need to be searching. It's got all the earmarks of a Mob-style hit, but the guy seems to be Mr.

Clean. Unless they're lying, Brady and his pumpkin weren't at Schroeder's place all day and I tend to believe them because of the .22. We need to dig deeper. There's got to be something in Schroeder's world that we can't see, yet."

Chapter Two

By mid-week we had the ballistics report, after the M.E. dug the bullet out of Robert Schroeder's brain. The bullet came from a .38 caliber, probably a snub-nosed, also called a Saturday night special.

I was in the office downing a morning decaf. Natalie had me off high-test coffee to help me stay calm. Since there was a Mob contract out on me last year, she felt that had added to my stress level. Imagine. I personally believe that a couple of good bourbons every day are more effective. From what I once read, Harry Truman had a shot at breakfast every morning. If it was good enough for Harry, it was good enough for me.

Around eight thirty, my desk phone rang. "Hello. Contino. Really. Okay, send him in."

A resident from Robert Schroder's condo complex was at the station and wanted to talk to the person in charge of the investigation. It wasn't uncommon for witnesses to clam up when officers are knocking on doors after a crime has been committed. They get a change of heart after a few days. This could be good news. Or not.

A small, elderly man, probably late seventies, came into my office area, an open room that I shared with three other people, including Jim Pearson. He stood in the doorway and spoke softly. "Detective Contino?" he said as if he was asking a question.

"That's me, sir. Please come in and have a seat." I stood up and motioned to the chair beside my desk. "Can I get you coffee or a glass of water?"

"No, thank you, Detective." He was in baggy gray slacks, a white shirt with a dark sweater vest over it. What hair he had was white, on all sides and back, typical male-pattern baldness. My day would come.

"What's your name, sir?"

"I'm Henry Driver, and I live in a townhouse near where that poor man was killed, just across from him."

"Why have you come in today, Mr. Driver?"

"When the officer knocked on my door that day, he asked if I saw anything strange or any people coming or going to that apartment. I didn't want to say anything at the time because I was scared and confused. I just wasn't sure what to do. I mean, if the killer knew I talked to the police, he might come after me. So I decided to wait a few days and then figured I'd better come here, rather than having the police show up at my place. I hope you're not mad at me."

"No, Mr. Driver. I'm not mad at you. In fact, I'm very happy that you had the courage to come here. Now, what is it that you want to say?"

"It might not be much, but I did see someone leave that apartment Sunday afternoon. It was around one o'clock and I was just looking out my front window, not at anything in particular and certainly not spying on anybody. I was just looking, you know, out the window. Well, I saw a man leaving the same apartment, the same one that had all the ruckus later on. You know, we've got a really nice complex. My daughter found this one for me. My wife died seven years ago, so I live alone."

"I'm sorry to hear about your wife. About this man, Mr. Driver. What did he look like?"

"He was tall, sort of, not as tall as you, Detective, but maybe three or four inches shorter. Of course, that's a lot taller than me. And he was a little heavy, especially around the middle. She was a great gal, my Lizzie. You would have liked her, Detective."

"I'm sure I would have, Mr. Driver. Tell me more about the man you saw. What color hair did he have? Could you see?"

"Oh, no. He was wearing a sweatshirt with a hood over his head. I couldn't really see him that well. Lizzie liked to wear sweatshirts."

I took a sip of my coffee. "Could you see his face? Did he have a beard?"

"No, no beard."

"Mr. Driver, could you see if he was a white man or a black man?"

"He was white, all right. No doubt about that. I knew a colored man once. He was a nice guy. Said he served in the Army, like me. That war sure was terrible. I don't blame these kids today, protesting against the new war. Terrible thing, just terrible."

"What about his clothes? What color were his clothes, Mr. Driver?"

"The sweatshirt was dark, like I said, bluish I'd say."

Mr. Driver went quiet after each brief answer. I took another drink of coffee.

"What about his pants, Mr. Driver?"

"His pants? I think he wore slacks. No, jeans, yes, blue jeans. They weren't shorts. No. Jeans. Lizzie never wore shorts, herself. I'm the only one who knows what great legs she had."

"What about his shoes? Could you see his shoes?"

"You know, I'm not sure. Oh, wait, yes. They were white. Yes, they were white, maybe like sneakers or something."

I paused while making notes. "So, you saw him leaving, a man in blue jeans with a dark blue sweatshirt, a hood over his head and white sneakers. Is that right?"

"Yes, sir. That's right." Mr. Driver sat up straight in his chair, pleased with his accounting of the events.

"What did he do next, Mr. Driver?"

"He left."

"Yes, he left. Of course. What kind of car did he have, Mr. Driver?"

"Car? Oh, there wasn't any car. No, sir. He walked away, down the sidewalk out to the main street."

I glanced at Jim Pearson, who avoided my gaze.

"Well, was there anything else that day, Mr. Driver, that you want to tell me about?"

Mr. Driver sat with his hands folded in his lap, looking down. "No, that's about it, Detective. That's all of it. That man in the sweatshirt, that's what I saw."

"Well, that's very helpful, Mr. Driver, very helpful."

Mr. Driver smiled at me. "I guess I did my civic duty all right, then. Yes, I did my duty. Lizzie always said we should do our civic duty."

"That's right, Mr. Driver, you certainly did. I'm very glad you came in today. Thank you very much."

Mr. Driver sat there smiling for a few seconds. Finally, he started getting up, nodding his head as he arose. "Yes, sir, a man in a dark sweatshirt, white shoes, that's who you should look for, Detective."

I walked Mr. Driver to the door of my office and aimed him at the building exit. His walk was light and springy. When I turned back into my office, Jim Pearson was grinning ear to ear.

"Knock it off, Jimbo. The guy did all right. He's a little slow in getting to the point, but he did all right."

"I agree. I just thought you had to pry it out of him a little."

"Hey, now we at least have something. There was definitely a man who visited Schroeder around early afternoon."

I checked with the lab boys and found out that there were no fingerprints other than those of the residents, but there were some faint prints on the floor, the kind that could have been left by boat shoes or tennis sneakers. This picture didn't exactly narrow things down much, but it was more than we had a few minutes ago, one small step.

"Jim, check that file of yours on old homicides. See if your newspaper clippings contain anything in the past year about a guy who fits the description Mr. Driver gave us. I'm going to give Leo a call and ask him to sniff around, too."

Jim Pearson kept a file of newspaper clippings and notes about homicides in Massachusetts that went back several years. It had paid off for us in the past.

Leo Barbado, my old partner and friend with the METs, now ran a private investigation business in Somerville. Among other benefits, it gave him some leverage in snooping around while off duty. I brought him up to speed on the Schroeder case and offered my usual compensation—a free trip to the Cape for a weekend of food and drink at my place. It always got him.

The female officer, Karen Orlando, who had helped Mrs. Schroeder, joined the department a few months after I came on board. She was bright, very attractive and eager to succeed. I know some of the guys were reluctant to accept a great-looking female, but I felt she had potential for more than just traffic duty. I wanted to get her involved with this case, believing that she would learn quickly and benefit from such an assignment. I had her check out Robert Schroeder and George Brady with the National Crime Information Center.

That came up dry. No prints or any criminal records on file. Brady was a low-life, if you asked me, but not that low. I didn't think he had the chutzpah to be a criminal, but it was worth a look.

That left us looking for a guy with a dark blue, hooded sweatshirt, blue jeans and white tennis shoes. At least it wasn't summer and he wasn't wearing a bathing suit with a hooded sweatshirt. Everybody on the Cape dresses like that.

The day was fruitless, and I was happy when quitting time arrived. When I got home, Nat was out. I remembered that it was her golf day with the girls. The bourbon bottle was on the hutch in the dining room, so I put some ice in a glass and treated myself to a drink. I dropped my coat on the sofa, kicked my shoes off and sat back in a recliner.

Halfway through my drink, I heard Nat's car pull into the driveway next to mine. She came into the house through the garage entrance and called to me.

"Hi, hon," she said. "How was your day?"

"Let's just say this is the best part of it."

"Well, of course it is, but I hoped you'd made some progress in your investigation."

"We did get a little more information from a neighbor of the victim, but nothing to write home about. How was golf?"

"It was about as good as your day. I didn't make much progress on my golf game, but we had fun."

Here was my gal, in her early fifties and still cutting a great figure in tight golf slacks and a sweater. She was smart and strong minded. She kept me anchored.

She appeared in the living room and approached my chair, sitting on the armrest. She put her arms around my neck and gave me a kiss on the cheek.

"I'm going to take a shower and then get dinner ready," she said, getting up and walking a few steps away. "Your drink looks good."

Nat quickly peeled off her sweater and then her bra. "Care for an appetizer, Detective?"

"You must be Bacall and I'm Bogie."

"She never did that, not on screen, anyway. She said something about whistling."

"I like your idea better."

Chapter Three

I was enjoying a night's sleep, at least I think I was, when the phone rang. I tried to get it before Nat woke up, but I failed.

"Sorry to roust you, Jack." It was Jim Pearson.

I rubbed my free hand over my face. "What's up? Christ, it's barely light out."

"Seems there was a B and E early this morning, about four o'clock."

"What's so fascinating about that, Jim? Can't the late shift handle it?"

His tone of voice said it all. "It was at West Dennis Liquors."

"I'll meet you there."

I got up, feeling groggy. You'd think I'd never done this before. "Christ." I washed up quickly, shaved and put on some casual clothes.

When I arrived, I parked in the lot that opened up in between stores on the south side of Main Street, also known as Route 28. The village was typical Cape Cod. All the stores on Main Street were one story, except a couple that had dormers added for a second story attic. They were covered by either white clapboard siding or weathered cedar shingles. The main entrance to the store faced the parking lot.

Two uniformed officers in addition to Pearson were there, one with a camera. He was snapping off pictures of the crime scene. The door was opened wide. Jim and I went in without touching it. The place smelled like a distillery.

"Hello, Jack," said the officer without the camera. It was Bill Davis, a tall, thin second-year cop who was working the night shift. "The thief smashed the door to get in, got into the register and cleaned it out. He smashed most of the bottles on the shelf behind the counter. He might have taken some, can't tell for sure."

"The thief," I said. "Only one?"

"Looks like one guy, because this is the only part of the store that's been disturbed. And it looks like just one set of prints. He left some good ones for us because of the spilled liquor. By the look of the tread, I'd say he was wearing tennis shoes."

I looked at Jim Pearson. He nodded.

"I think you're right, Bill, but he didn't clean out the register. This store's been closed for a few days. The owner was the murder victim last Sunday. His assistant cleaned the cash out before closing up Sunday and locked it in a safe in the back room. Check it out."

Davis was gone for a minute, while Pearson and I looked around. The smell was strong, so we decided to step outside.

"The safe looks intact, still locked," said Davis when he returned. "They have a security camera, but it records onto a tape and they forgot to change it since the last one ran out, so that's no help."

"Bill, I don't suppose there were any witnesses around at four o'clock."

"Actually, there's a breakfast diner across the street and the owner was in there with his wife, baking. His name is Joseph Cohen. I told him to be expecting you."

"Thanks. Jim, help Bill finish up here. I'll go see the Cohens."

I was wearing a blue windbreaker over a white golf shirt, but there was a morning chill lingering in the Cape air, so I turned the collar up as I walked across the quiet street to the diner. The place was dimly lit and I couldn't read the sign in the window until I got up close, "Cohen's." *Simple enough,* I thought.

I knocked on the front door and it opened immediately. Mr. Cohen stood there, a small man, about sixty, with a white baker's apron, matching the color of his sparse hair. His wife was across the room in the kitchen area, going about her business of getting the place ready for the breakfast business. It was mid-September and the tourists were gone, but the locals frequented this place, including me. I had never talked to Mr. Cohen before, other than a quick hello when picking up a coffee and muffin. I wasn't exactly a regular, but his coffee was much better than that at the station house, so I stopped by a couple of times a week.

"Hello, Detective Contino. So that's your name. We never get to talk, but I see you in here now and then. This is a heck of a way to meet." He extended his small hand and we shook. "Come in, come in."

He motioned me to a table near the door, which he closed and locked behind us. I took my seat, opened my jacket a bit and took out a small notepad and pen.

"What a noise that alarm at the liquor store makes," he said. "When it went off, I didn't know what to think at first. We've got one here, too, but you never expect to hear one. Shirley and I were making the muffins and donuts and then, all of a sudden, that alarm. Say, I hope you don't mind if Shirley keeps working. We've got to get ready. Besides, she didn't see anything. When the alarm went off, I told her to stay in the back while I looked out."

"I understand, Mr. Cohen. What did you see?"

"As I said, I ran to the door and looked out the glass. The parking lot is pretty well lit all night. At first, nothing. Then after a couple minutes, a guy comes out. He's got his arms around something, probably some bottles, and he runs away through the back of the parking lot."

"Could you tell what he looked like?"

"He looked husky and a little tall."

"What do you mean, Mr. Cohen?"

"Well, Detective, I don't think as tall as you, but much bigger than me."

"Did you see what he was wearing?"

"No, not really. I couldn't make that out. Everything he had on was dark, even in the light, and he ran, so I didn't get a good look. He just seemed to have on a top that covered his head."

"Like a hooded sweatshirt, maybe?"

"Yes, yes, that could be."

"And you say he ran away. He didn't drive?"

"No, Detective. He ran to the back of the parking lot, away from the light. I guess he was in a hurry, what with the alarm going off, he knew the cops were coming soon. There's a fence at the back of the lot. He must have gone over that or maybe through an opening. Say, Detective, isn't that awful? Poor Bob Schroeder gets killed and then his store gets robbed, too. Poor Anne. She must be in a terrible state."

"So you know the Schroeders."

"Sure, we're business neighbors here in town. They came in here every day, but later than you, since they don't open until ten. Nice people, the Schroeders."

"Did you ever meet the partner, George Brady? I understand that he and Mr. Schroeder had a falling out over the business."

"Oh, they had a falling out, all right. Sometimes I'd be in the store when they were arguing. But I'm not so sure it was about the business."

"How's that? What do you mean?"

"Well, I think Mrs. Schroeder got along with George a little too well. One time, I saw him give her a pat on the tuchus and she didn't seem to mind at all."

Mr. Cohen looked around to see where Shirley was, then curled his finger up and motioned me in closer to him. "Actually," he whispered, "I guess it lasted a little too long to be a friendly pat. But I should mind my own business. It was probably nothing."

"So, Mr. Cohen, you think Robert knew about these pats or maybe there was more going on?"

"I don't know, Detective, like I said, it was probably nothing."

"Do you recall anything specific that Robert might have said to George about it?"

"No, I don't. I just wouldn't be surprised if that was part of the arguments, that's all."

"Okay, Mr. Cohen, thanks."

Mr. Cohen took a breath and shook his head. "Who would want to do these terrible things to them?"

"I don't know, Mr. Cohen, but I'm sure going to find out. So, it was just the one man you saw?"

"That's correct, just one. I sure hope you catch him and the killer, too. Say, do you think it could be the same man, both times?"

"I'm going to find out, Mr. Cohen. Believe me, I'm going to find out. Thanks for all your help. If you think of anything else, give me a call." I put my pen and pad away and handed him my card.

"I certainly will, Detective. I certainly will."

I jogged across the street and met up with Jim Pearson and Bill Davis. "Mr. Cohen saw a man who might have been wearing a hooded sweatshirt run out of the store and into the darkness back there." I pointed to the back area of the lot. "When it gets light, check it out for footprints and a trail and take it as far as it leads."

"Will do, Jack," said Bill.

I was starting to feel empty in the gut, in need of some breakfast. "I'm heading home to freshen up and get a bite. See you in the office later."

Could it be possible that the same guy who killed Schroeder would try to rob his store a few days later? It didn't seem possible. It didn't make sense. There was too much risk. One crime looked like a well-planned, professional hit. The other looked like an amateur smash-and-grab job. I'd never seen the likes of this before.

Chapter Four

At home, I caught Nat in mid-yawn as I walked into the kitchen and checked to see if there was fresh coffee. No problem. Nat had just brewed a new pot and was downing a cup herself.

"After all these years, you'd think I'd get used to those middle of the night calls, Jack, but I haven't." Nat was in a white terrycloth robe and green slippers, sitting at the breakfast table, a bowl of cereal in front of her. She liked fruit on her cereal, so she scattered some blueberries across the top. I guess she was just getting started.

"Did you get back to sleep?" I asked.

"Not really, but I can't eat at four in the morning, so I showered and read a book for a while. Now that it's about five-thirty, I decided I was ready for breakfast, so I got the coffee going and poured myself some cereal, some honey nut crunchy things that the grandkids like. They're good, if you can get past the bright colors. Are you hungry?"

"Yes, indeed. I could stand some scrambles and bacon, with toast and coffee." I realized too late that I made it sound like I was placing an order.

"Yes, sir. Can I wash your car while I'm at it?"

"Hon, I didn't mean for you . . ."

"Oh, relax, Jack. I'm just busting your chops a bit. Of course I'll fix you breakfast. Go shower and change."

What's that phrase the shrinks like to call a guy's family, his *support system?* That was Nat all right. She kept me upright for a long time, through all kinds of hell.

I took a quick shower. As I toweled off, I checked myself in the door mirror. The scar on my gut still looked pretty ugly, but at least I was around to see it. The bullet came from hit man Ben Secani's Berretta a few years earlier. It put me down, but not out. I managed to squeeze off my service revolver from my knees that night and put an end to his story. He would have killed his call girl friend, Maria

Falcone that night, too, since he learned I had her turn snitch for me. When Secani turned to shoot at her, it gave me the chance to nail him. She took a shot in the leg for her trouble. I guess we saved each other that night.

I ran my finger over the scar, tracing the incision. The bullet did a nasty job internally and I cursed out loud as I looked at the reflection in the mirror. It took me a couple of months before I was back on the job after that hit. Nat wanted me to quit immediately, take a medical retirement, but I couldn't. I still wanted a chance to nail Tommy Shea and all the rotten bastards who worked with him.

I dressed and joined Natalie in the kitchen. She was sitting at the table, sipping her coffee. A plate with my breakfast was waiting on the table with a cover over it and a tall mug of coffee beside it. The mug was my first target.

"Jack, is everything okay?" asked Nat. "I thought I heard you groaning in the shower, something maybe related to that old wound?"

"Naw. I was just checking it out and cursing the bastard who did it. I'm fine."

"That's what I expect you to say, but, you know, you're due for a complete physical. I want you to get one right away . . . and I won't take no for an answer."

"Aw, Nat, I'm fine."

"Don't 'aw, Nat' me. I want you to get a full checkup. I'll make the call and set it up. No argument, get it?"

"Yeah, okay. I know you're right, Nurse Ratched. If it'll make you happy, I'll do it." She gave me that look that says *I won.*

I got back to the office around eight. Jim wasn't back yet. He must have followed my routine, getting cleaned up and changed into uniform.

I called Anne Schroeder at her sister's house to tell her what was going on. She struggled against tears as I spoke.

"Why? Why is this happening to us? This is the cruelest coincidence I've ever heard of. What am I going to do?"

"Mrs. Schroeder, it's possible that it's not a coincidence. It's possible that your husband's killer might have decided to try robbing the store. He'd know that it would be closed for a while and he probably thought there'd still be money in the cash register and it would be an easy score."

"Oh, my God, that's unbelievable. What kind of animal is this?" Her sobs became louder.

"We're not certain about this, Mrs. Schroeder, but there was a witness, Mr. Cohen across the street."

"Yes, I know him."

"He saw a man leave the store after the alarm went off. From what Mr. Cohen could tell me, he resembled a man seen leaving your townhouse last Sunday."

"You have a witness at the killing? What did he see?"

"Mrs. Schroeder, I can't tell you any more than that. Please keep this close to the vest, but I thought you should know." I was going against my better judgment, telling her this much, but I wanted to help ease her pain. I'm not sure I succeeded.

"Of course, Detective, and I appreciate your telling me this much. I'm glad to hear that you have a lead, something to work with." She became calm, almost as if she was trying to give me encouragement. "I'll go to the store as soon as I can and I'll call the insurance company. I assume you have officers still there?"

"Yes, Mrs. Schroeder. I'll tell them to expect you. We're going to do everything we can to help you."

After we hung up, I could still hear the desperation in her voice when she first spoke. I began to think I had some idea what Nat must have felt when she got the call about my being shot. I hated that I ever put her through that.

Jim Pearson came into the office shortly after I got off the phone with Mrs. Schroeder. He had freshened up after the early start to the day. "We found some footprints, as you expected, Jack. There was a dirt lot beyond the fence and we could see a trail where the grass and weeds have been worn away into a path, probably by locals in that neighborhood behind the stores. Anyway, it ran up to a street, but ended there on the road shoulder. There were some tire marks that looked fresh. I guess he parked his car there to avoid detection."

"Are the tire marks clear enough to make a plaster cast? If so, we might at least be able to ID the tires." The tires were a long shot, but it might allow us to narrow down the type of car the thief had used. I didn't think he'd be a full-time pedestrian.

"I don't know, but we can try. I'll get right on it."

"Good. And Jim, Mrs. Schroeder will be going to the store, so let the guys know."

"Will do, Jack. By the way, Henry Santino was at the scene just before I left. He has an office around the block and was showing up for work. He didn't have anything to offer. He said the same things about Schroeder that we've heard so far, a good guy, no enemies that he knew of, didn't care for his ex-partner. I told him we'd get in touch again if we needed to."

Chapter Five

After a week, his sweatshirt wreaked of stale booze since he hadn't washed it yet. The smell was starting to bother him, so he decided to go to the coin operated laundry. After stuffing it in a pillowcase along with the clothes that were piled up in his bedroom, he grabbed some coins and paper money and walked out of his small, basement apartment in Hyannis. Slinging the pillowcase over his shoulder, he made the short walk back to Main Street. The cool evening air felt good in his nostrils, a stark contrast to his apartment.

The young man walked into the laundry and had plenty of machines to choose from, since there were only two other people there. One was a black woman, an older woman by his twenty-something standards, loading a dryer. The other was a much younger white girl, younger than him, probably. She was sitting on a bench facing the machines and was reading a hardcover book, holding it up with both hands. She had on a red turtleneck sweater and blue jeans that were tight against her thighs. She had long, light brown hair, which he liked. Some of it fell casually over her right eye and she brushed it back once. She was pretty enough, but her small chest disappointed him.

He picked a machine next to the one the young girl was using and loaded his laundry into it. Looking around, he spotted the soap vending machines and strolled up to them, fishing money out of his pockets as he walked. As he crossed in front of the girl, he noticed a label on the bottom of the spine of the book with alpha numeric characters on it and the letters CCCC under them. *Must be a library book from Cape Cod Community College,* he thought.

After starting his wash, he moved over to the bench. The girl instinctively slid to one end, away from him, even though the bench could easily sit four adults and he wasn't trying to crowd her. He sat just past the center of the bench, away from her, putting his hands on the bench seat, and relaxed against the back rest.

The husky young man let curiosity get the better of him and he stole a glance at the girl and her book, noting the title, *Criminal Investigation*. He was impressed. *That's pretty heavy stuff for a girl.*

"Excuse me, are you going to be a cop? That's a tough gig for a girl... woman, you know. Good luck with that."

He saw her give him a quick glance and then return to her book.

"I mean, good luck, really. I think that's great."

She spoke without dropping the book. "Thanks. Women can go into law enforcement, you know. There are lots of women in police departments."

"Yeah, I know. I've seen some here in Hyannis. Nothing wrong with that."

"I'm glad you approve." She lowered the book to get a better look at the man. "Actually, I plan to go on to a four year college, probably UMass Boston and then go to law school. I want to be a criminal lawyer."

"No kidding. Hey, that's really great. You know exactly what you want to do. That's great."

She nodded and went back to her book, signaling the end of the conversation, as far as she was concerned.

He tapped his fingers on the bench and looked around the room. The black woman was still there. *Too bad.*

"So, you live around here?"

She waited before answering. "Actually, I live in Worcester and I come here to this laundry twice a month."

"Hey, you don't have to get snitty about it."

"Oh please. Stop right there. I don't need a come on from some guy in a laundromat."

"Look, I wasn't coming on or nothing. I was just making conversation, okay? Just conversation."

"All right, I'm sorry. I didn't mean to be rude, but I don't want to make conversation. I'm trying to read my assignment, that's all. I'm sure you can understand."

"Yeah, sure, of course I can understand." *I understand that you're a conceited bitch.*

Her dryer stopped and she sprang off the bench to fetch it.

Saved by the bell, huh, bitch.

She grabbed her clothes and threw them into a two-wheeled basket with a long handle, not bothering to check the load for dryness. In a flash she was out the door.

He watched her go, his mouth shut tight. He turned his head and saw the black woman giving him a quick glance. She turned back to her task as soon as his eyes caught hers.

You old bitch. You'd just love it if I'd give you a tussle, wouldn't you, horny old bitch. Mind your own business. Go fuck yourself.

Later, when the black woman was gone and he was watching his clothes spinning in the dryer, he thought about the girl and her book.

CCCC. I bet there's a lot of conceited bitches there. Bunch of college girls think they're hot shit. CCCC. Yeah, bet there are lots of them, lots to pick from. Yeah.

Chapter Six

Cape Cod full timers loved it after Labor Day. The summer residents were gone, with kids back in school, and the weekend crowds were much smaller, too. You could drive anywhere without running into heavy traffic. Even Route 28, the bane of every motorist's existence during the summer, was a breeze, except near the Hyannis airport. The rotary always seemed to slow things down.

I thought about that comment from Mr. Cohen about George Brady and Anne Schroeder being too friendly. I needed to follow up on that tidbit. Besides, it was almost two weeks since the murder, and I wanted to see how she was doing. After trying unsuccessfully to reach her by phone a couple of times, and having no other leads to pursue, I decided to drive to Sandwich.

I took Route 6, the Mid-Cape Highway, to the exit at Route 130. Sandwich is a great little town, very colonial, it's the oldest incorporated town on the Cape. Natalie wanted to buy a house there, but the taxes kept me looking elsewhere, and I wanted to be closer to the Dennis PD headquarters. She came around to my way of thinking. Score one for me.

I found Anne Schroeder's sister's address in a nice, quiet neighborhood just off Route 130, near the new high school. The street was lined with old oak trees and the properties, roughly half acre lots, were well-landscaped. There was an oval driveway in front, a nice idea, so I pulled in and parked right at the front door, went up to it and rang the bell. I got a response on the second ring. A woman nearly identical to Anne, but a bit older, answered the door.

"I'm Detective Jack Contino from the Dennis Police. Are you Anne Schroeder's sister?"

"Yes, Detective, I'm Barbara Erikson. She's mentioned your name often. Please come in."

"Is Anne here? I'd like to speak with her, to see how she's doing, you know."

"Oh, no, Detective, she's not here right now. She's with her lawyer. I believe they were meeting at the store. He's an old family friend and they're going over some plans to get the store reopened. I'm afraid I don't expect her for a while."

Mrs. Erikson led me to the living room, where we sat down in nicely upholstered chairs at an angle to one another, a small table with a shaded lamp separating them. She offered me a drink, I said no. "You know, Detective, it still seems impossible to believe that Bob is gone. It makes you wonder, if this can happen to Bob, is anybody safe from these people?"

"From these people?"

"Yes, you know, criminals."

I looked down at my feet for a second and almost bit my lip. "How's she been doing? Is she holding up all right?"

"Yes, under the circumstances. She's a strong girl, Detective. My little sister has strength and courage. She always did."

"Yes, I got that sense when I talked to her the first time. She told me about Mr. Schroeder's business partner, George Brady. Did you know him?"

Mrs. Erikson looked at me a little uneasy as she spoke. "Yes, of course, I met George many times over the years."

"What did you know about him, Mrs. Erikson?"

"You don't think he had anything to do with this, do you?

"I just have to cover all the bases, Mrs. Erikson. I know he and Mr. Schroeder were friends and had a falling out. Do you know anything about that?"

Mrs. Erikson paused a moment, as if she needed to contemplate her answer very carefully.

"It was a business disagreement. I know that."

I waited before speaking. "Was there anything else that might have contributed to their differences, anything at all?"

"Detective, let me ask you a question. When you find the killer and there is a trial, will I have to testify at all?"

"That's hard to say at this point. Why do you ask?"

"Well, I just wonder if I might be called as a character witness or something like that."

"As I said, I can't know that right now, Mrs. Erikson. That's a question you'll have to ask the District Attorney."

"I see. I guess I should tell you this, although I don't want to make more trouble for Anne." She spoke more slowly. "Three years ago, she had an affair with George Brady. It didn't last long, but while it was going on, she said George would get too playful with her."

"Meaning what, playful in what way?"

"He'd flirt with her in front of Bob, touching her shoulder, putting his arm around her and when Bob wasn't around, he'd fondle her. At first, she didn't mind, but then he'd do it when customers were in the store. She was certain people could see that and she told him to stop. She was afraid Bob would find out, or worse, even see him doing it. Bob didn't like the flirting and thought it went too far and he told George to cut it out."

"What was George's reaction?"

"He laughed it off and told Bob it was nothing, that they were just old friends, and that he shouldn't be so sensitive. That's when Anne broke off the affair. George got angry and I guess that's why they started arguing more and more, always saying it was about the business. Obviously, there was more to it than that."

"To your knowledge, Mrs. Erikson, did either of them ever threaten each other?"

"No, not that I know. Sometimes, they got very loud. They'd usually be in the back office at the store, but Anne said you could hear them out front near the register. But I don't think there were any physical threats. Detective, I hope I'm not causing more trouble. I don't want to make things worse, but if there's a chance I'd have to testify, I didn't want you to think I was hiding anything. I hope you won't tell Anne about this."

"Mrs. Erikson, your sister hasn't been forthright with me. I'm going to have to talk with her and try to get her to open up about the affair. I'll try to get her to do it on her own, without telling her about our conversation, but I can't make any promises. You've done the right thing, Mrs. Erikson. This gives me reason to talk to George Brady again, too."

"You think he did it, don't you?"

"I don't know. I'm not ruling him out. It wouldn't be the first time a love affair led to murder. I have to dig a lot deeper, that's all."

"I understand, Detective." Barbara Erikson's eyes began to glaze over. I think it was a combination of fatigue and emotional pain. But she sat straight up in her chair, sitting near the edge. "This whole thing is just so awful."

I thanked Mrs. Erikson for her help and let myself out. I made some notes in my pad when I got into my car. After starting the engine, I looked at the front window of the living room, but there was nobody looking out. I guess she'd seen enough of me for now.

Chapter Seven

I drove to West Dennis, hoping to catch Mrs. Schroeder at her store. The sky was turning cloudy and it looked like a shower was possible. On the Cape, however, the weather changed quickly. Sometimes the storms developed and sometimes they didn't.

After arriving in West Dennis, I parked in the lot outside the store and walked over to the fence to see the spot where the robber fled. It was just an impulse and I knew I wouldn't make any great discovery, but something drew me to his getaway path. I guess it was a way of feeling a connection.

The store door had multiple panes of glass on the top half, so I could see inside. Knocking on it brought a man out of a back room. I assumed he was the lawyer. Standing in the door arch, he looked at me and then turned back to Mrs. Schroeder. He stepped back as she appeared, looked, and moved toward me, turning her head back to the man and saying something.

She opened the door and greeted me.

"Hello, Mrs. Schroeder, may I come in?"

"Detective, what's happened? Do you have some new information about Robert's killer?"

"No, I wanted to see how you are doing. I haven't heard from you for over a week."

"That's very nice of you, Detective Contino, but I'm fine. Thank you for stopping by. I appreciate your concern."

"Mrs. Schroeder, I really need to talk to you, privately."

The man was walking toward us.

"Is there a problem?" he asked. "I'm Winton Carlson, Mrs. Schroeder's friend and attorney."

"No, Winton, there's no problem. Detective Contino is in charge of the investigation. He just wants to talk to me."

"Perhaps I should stay with you."

"That's not necessary, Mr. Carlson. Mrs. Schroeder's not a suspect. I need to talk to her about someone who might be."

Mrs. Schroeder moved toward the back room, a small office with a brown desk plus matching chair, and waved me in. "There's no need for you to stay, Winton. Go get a cup of coffee across the street. I'm sure we'll just be a few minutes."

The lawyer exhaled, shrugged his shoulders and did as he was told. I wondered if she always had him on a leash.

Mrs. Schroeder was wearing tight-fitting blue slacks and a white T-shirt under a yellow hooded sweatshirt. Normally a hooded sweatshirt wouldn't be at all unusual, but this time it felt eerily ironic. She took a seat at a desk that was against a side wall. I pulled up a small wooden chair from the corner.

"What is it you want to talk about, Detective? Is it about George Brady? Isn't he the one you think is a suspect?"

"I haven't learned anything else about him, Mrs. Schroeder. I was wondering if there was any more that you could tell me."

"Well, Detective, I really don't know what else I can say about him. I think I've covered it, you know, his relationship with Bob."

"Yes, but, I was wondering about how you saw him. What were his likes, his dislikes, things like that?"

"He was pretty easy going, for as long as I knew him, until his arguments with Bob started. He liked good food, and bad food, for that matter. Beer, he liked beer, too."

"What about women? He was single, wasn't he?"

Mrs. Schroeder stiffened slightly.

"Yes, he was single. He dated a lot. He never seemed to stay with one girl for very long. He was a true swinging bachelor, I guess."

"Was he well-behaved around women?"

"What do you mean, Detective?" She folded her arms across her chest.

"Was he a gentleman, for example, or something else?"

"He wasn't exactly what I'd call a gentleman. He didn't dress that well and he was a bit dumpy, you know, a little overweight with bad posture. No, he definitely didn't fit the bill as a gentleman. He could be a flirt. Whenever we had a party he'd bring a date, but he would work the room, you know, checking out the other women. He always seemed to be touching them, a hand on the shoulder or back or arm."

Mrs. Schroeder's eyes went skyward as she talked, as if she were having a personal memory.

"Did he act like that with you, Mrs. Schroeder?"

Her eyes came back to earth, first making contact with me, and then turning to one side. "Well, we were old friends, of course, so I guess I didn't pay any attention to it, but, yes, he'd touch me like that from time to time."

"Was that all? Did he ever try to touch you in a different way?"

Her lips came together and her face grew taut. She looked like the cat who swallowed the canary. She didn't answer.

"Did he ever come on to you, Mrs. Schroeder?"

"What are you getting at, Detective? He was a friend." She made a half turn away from me. I think she wanted to run away if she could.

"Mrs. Schroeder, I need to know everything I can about your husband, George Brady and you. The circle around this case is very small."

"Sometimes, Detective, George and I . . . got close. He had genuine affection for me and I for him. We knew each other for a long time." She swallowed hard. "Sometimes . . . he would put his hand on me and caress me. We were friends. It was all right."

"Did it become more than just all right, Mrs. Schroeder?"

She turned back toward me. Her expression said her secret was out.

"Robert was always so busy with the store and making plans for the business. He would be out at meetings with realtors and looking for other store possibilities, not to mention the late hours at the store. George made me feel like I was wanted. After a while, I guess I returned his affection with caresses of my own. He started touching me more intimately, and I liked it."

She paused and her voice cracked as she spoke.

"Yes, yes, we had an affair. Isn't that what you wanted to hear? I'm not proud of it, but I gave in."

"What happened, Mrs. Schroeder?"

"Do you want me to paint you a picture? Is that what you want?"

"No, Mrs. Schroeder, that's not what I meant."

She regained her composure and continued.

"After a while, I realized that George didn't really feel strongly about me. I was like those dates he'd go out with. It was just lust. He'd squeeze me every chance he could, but there was no caring in it. My body was just a toy for him and it was available for a feel almost every day. So, I broke off the affair. He didn't like that. And I think Bob had gotten wise to us. I'm certain he must have seen George groping me, and I didn't resist. They began having arguments about the business. At first they were more like discussions, but then they became shouting matches. Our behavior, George and mine, must have fueled those arguments. Finally, George said he wanted out and that led to Bob agreeing to a buyout. You know the rest."

"You realize that you've just made George a more solid suspect."

"I thought you said you didn't think he did it?"

"Based on what I knew before, I didn't, but love triangles are sometimes a motive for murder. Brady's an unlikely suspect, but a suspect just the same."

"You're wrong, Detective, I'm sure you are."

"Has he contacted you since the killing?"

"No. Come to think of it, he didn't even come to the funeral, or at least I didn't see him and, if he was there, he never approached me."

I didn't want to continue this ordeal for her. "Thank you, Mrs. Schroeder, I appreciate your cooperation. I promise you we'll find your husband's killer and whoever robbed your store."

She looked up at me and tears filled her eyes; her hands clasped tightly together. If she had been holding something, like a pencil, she would have broken it. She said nothing as I left. She'd have to answer to her own conscience.

Chapter Eight

The campus of Cape Cod Community College is on a hill in West Barnstable, just north of the intersection of Route 6 and Route 132. A series of parking lots surround the hill, upon which sit the classroom buildings, science building, administration building and the library.

It was around four o'clock when the man, wearing his favorite dark blue, hooded sweatshirt, drove into the parking lot. It was a gray, overcast day. Most of the students had gone home for the day and he had no problem finding a place for his car. After parking, he saw a concrete stairway on the hill and headed for it. At the top of the stairs, he paused to look around. Seeing some coeds going into the library, a few yards ahead of where he stood, he decided to start his search there.

As he entered the library, the main desk for checking out materials was on his left. He continued deeper into the open room. A stairway at the back of the room led to the other floors, including the basement level. He chose the basement for exploration, didn't find much activity there, then returned to the main floor. Turning to his right at the top of the stairs, he circled through the reference section. Students sat with books open and hands busily writing in notebooks. He checked out the girls. Some wore cargo pants that looked like they were designed for house painters or carpenters. Some had tight jeans. He wasn't impressed. As he worked his way close to the check-out desk, he saw her.

A young woman, perhaps in her early thirties, stood at the desk talking to an elderly woman on the other side. She wore a tight gray skirt, cut just above her knees, exposing perfect legs. She had on a delicate looking white blouse, with a lace pattern running along the edge where it buttoned. Her breasts pushed the blouse out to a fullness that made him smile and her hair was shoulder length, light brown. He swallowed hard.

The woman talked for several minutes, and the man decided to move around the room slowly to avoid being noticed, but never losing sight of his target. When she finally ended her conversation, she walked briskly out of the building and the man followed at a safe distance. He kept pace with her as she cut across the campus, past the first classroom building. She reached the next building and entered through doors at the far right. He hurried to keep her in sight.

He lost her when she climbed the stairs to the second level. The stairs went halfway to the top and had a landing where they switched back. There was another landing with a door at the top, leading into the section with a central lobby and office rooms on both sides, running the length of the building. The walls were unpainted cinder block, a pattern broken by occasional paintings, posters and bulletin boards. He stopped just inside the lobby, his eyes and ears searching for her. Students sat on sofas, some alone and some with friends. Some were reading. Some were talking. *Welcome to community college, kiddies, a great big babysitting service. Glad I never wasted my time here.*

He decided to walk to his right and take a course that brought him a few feet outside of each office door. He glanced into each office as he passed by.

The first office had an older-looking man with plastic-rimmed glasses sitting at his desk reading a stack of papers, probably student work, he thought. *Making a nice living here, Pops? Yeah, the Commonwealth will take care of you.*

He continued on, glancing at bulletin boards and posters between offices. The next one was empty. Then he heard female voices. He flipped the hood of his sweatshirt up and looked into the next office, slowing his steps to get a long look. She was there, standing with her back to the door, talking with another woman sitting at a desk. *Pay dirt.*

He circled back, making a left turn and moving to a chair across the lobby that gave him a clear view of her. *What a body. This could be great, a teacher, too. I don't want one of those conceited little college bitches, anyway. She's got the goods.* He rubbed his crotch.

He sat forward in the chair, flipping through some magazines that lay on a table in front of him, periodically glancing up at her. When she shifted her weight onto one foot, her body moved in a way that made him clench his teeth. When she ended her conversation, she picked up a big brown purse and strapped it over her left shoulder, clutching a large notebook against her ample chest. *Those lucky books. Don't worry, old boy, you're going to get there soon enough. You have a new mission. This is going to keep that bastard busy.*

She moved quickly to the same door she'd entered, and he followed casually behind. As she exited the building, he moved faster, shortening the distance between them while they headed down the stairs leading to the parking lot. He wanted a good look at her car.

Her red Mercury Cougar had vanity plates on it that read, "ENGLISH." *Thanks for the help, lady. That's as good as a bulls eye.*

Their cars were at least one hundred yards apart, so he jogged to his while she dropped her purse, placed her notebook on the hood of the car and dug out her keys. He pulled his keys out of his sweatshirt pocket as he ran and had them ready when he reached his car. He drove to where her Cougar had been parked, but it was gone. His car turned onto the driveway that circled the campus, leading to the exit on Route 132. He looked to his right and caught a glimpse of the red Cougar well down the road, so he pressed hard on the gas pedal to close the distance. She approached the end of the road, where the only choices were to turn east or west on Route 6-A. *Please live in Dennis, pretty lady, or I'm going to have to take you there. Be a good girl.*

It was easy to keep the red Cougar in sight as they meandered down 6-A, through Barnstable and into Yarmouth Port. *Closer. Closer.*

Her Cougar slowed down in Dennis and turned right onto Signal Hill Drive. *Fantastic. This is my lucky day.* He closed in on her and saw her turn left onto Courier Drive. He followed slowly into the cul-de-sac and watched her pull into the driveway of a weathered shingled ranch house. He kept going, grinning from ear to ear, and drove to the next street off Signal Hill where he parked his car, grabbed a backpack from the passenger seat and cut back through a wooded lot to her house. *This is going to be so freakin' great.*

Chapter Nine

Tina Johnson answered the door with her usual chunk of bad attitude when I arrived at George Brady's house in the late afternoon with a search warrant, accompanied by Sergeant Pearson, Officer Orlando and Officer Davis.

She opened the door wide enough for us to get a good look at her. She was wearing a dark blue T-shirt that had a front pocket. That was it. What was under the shirt was anybody's guess. Her legs were as tanned as her face and arms.

"Oh, no, not you again. Now what?"

"Nice to see you again, too, Miss Johnson. I have a warrant to search the premises." I didn't wait for her to open the door wider. I used my size to make the point that we were coming in, whether she liked it or not.

"Hey, make yourself comfortable, Detective. Why don't you just break the damned door down, while you're at it?"

The other officers followed me in and I motioned with one hand for them to spread out into the house and commence the search. At the same time, I took the warrant out of my coat pocket with the other hand and held it out for Miss Johnson. She didn't look at it, turning away with her hands on her hips, spinning a short circle, like a dog before it sits down. Then she thrust her hands out to her sides, palms up.

"What the hell is this for? George can't be a suspect in your murder. You know he was here with me when that happened."

"Yes, we know you told us that." I looked around as I spoke, in case George made a surprise appearance.

"Oh, so you think I'm lying? What about the gun? He showed you his gun. What else are you expecting to find, hand grenades or something?"

"Speaking of George, where is he?"

"He's not here, okay? He had something to do. I don't know. I don't nag him about his personal business. Are you going to tell me what the hell are you looking for?"

"That's none of your concern, Miss Johnson. Please just stay out of the way while we conduct the search."

Unlike what you see on television, we don't make a mess of the place when we do a search. We try to be as orderly as possible. If you just toss stuff around, you can't always tell what areas have been searched and which haven't, so you try to restore a searched area to its original condition, always working a room from one side to the other. If we take things out of a dresser drawer, we put them back. If we lift hanging clothes off a closet rack, we put them back.

According to the warrant, we were searching for the possible murder weapon, a .38 caliber revolver. George could have put his .22 on display to throw us off. It made sense, if he was the killer.

Officers Davis and Orlando searched the master bedroom. Bill took out the dresser drawers one by one, placing them on the bed, and Karen went through the contents. There was no obvious sign of a gun, so Bill checked the structure of the dresser, in case there was a hidden compartment. No dice.

"Hey, you mind if I put on some shorts? I'm not dressed for company," said Tina, who started for the bedroom.

"Please wait right there, Miss Johnson, until we're finished. Why don't you take a seat here?" I motioned to the sofa while I made my search through the TV cabinet. She made a noise showing her displeasure with my recommendation, like a kid being disciplined by a parent, and took a seat at one end of the sofa, sitting upright, folding her arms across her chest and crossing her legs.

We took our time with the house search, not wanting to skip any places where a gun could be hidden, but we came up empty in the end. I needed to search his car as well, so I'd need another warrant and a return visit for that. I didn't tell that to Tina Johnson, who was now stretched out on the sofa, showing a lot of leg and not making any effort to cover herself.

"We're done, Miss Johnson. Thank you for your cooperation," I said.

"Are you satisfied, Detective?"

"Not entirely. I need to talk to Mr. Brady again. When do you expect him?"

"Like I said, I don't know. I don't check him in and out." She didn't get off the sofa as we left.

Jim Pearson walked beside me as we made our way back to our cars. "I know you were hoping for an open-and-shut case, Jack. Aren't we all? But until we find the murder weapon, I guess this one stays open."

"I'm afraid so. Then we just keep on working it."

"And we didn't even find a blue hooded sweatshirt or white tennis shoes," he said.

"Which means he could be wearing them right now."

Davis and Orlando had gotten into their cruiser, while Jim and I stopped for a moment next to my car and looked back at the house. George Brady hadn't been up front with us about Anne Schroeder. Of course, she hadn't been either. Was there any more about this case that they were holding back?

I heard the police radio squawking from Bill's cruiser, while I eased my way into the driver's seat of my car. As I started the engine, Bill got out of his car and ran up to mine, so I rolled down the driver's side window.

"Jack, there's been a murder over in Dennis, near Route 6-A. It's real bad."

Chapter Ten

With lights flashing and the sirens blaring, we raced to the address Officer Davis gave me, with him in the lead. It was late afternoon and the sky was growing cloudy again.

The cul-de-sac was filling up with vehicles. Three other police cruisers were already there, along with a fire department rescue truck with the EMTs. The medical examiner had not arrived yet. Residents were emerging from their houses to peek at the commotion that disturbed their usually quiet street. A bright red Cougar was deep into the driveway and a green Volkswagen bug was behind it.

An officer met me and Jim Pearson at the front door to the house. Officers Davis and Orlando stood behind, allowing me to go first. Seniority has its privileges and responsibilities.

The officer stood in the doorway with a notepad in his hands, which were shaking.

"What have we got, officer?"

"It's pretty bad, Detective, a white female, about thirty to thirty-five years of age. Her name is Blake Hairston. She teaches at the community college. Her live-in boyfriend found her when he came home from work. He's sitting with an officer over there." The officer pointed to the man who was seated on a sofa, his head buried in his hands. "He thinks he spooked the killer into fleeing the scene early, but he didn't see him."

"Fleeing early? What do you mean, officer? I'm not following you."

The officer's voice cracked as he talked.

"I'm sorry, Detective. I've never seen anything so brutal in my life."

"Calm down, son. Just tell me the details. Take your time. We're not going anywhere." For a minute, I thought I was going to have to hold him up.

"Sir, the woman . . . the victim, she's in the bathtub, naked and . . . cut up. I mean, he was dismembering her, sir. Her feet, her legs, her hands, have all been cut off. I don't know how anybody . . ."

I looked at Jim Pearson. His mouth was open, with a look of disbelief. Homicides were rare in Dennis, until I came to town. This was the second one in less than a month and the third since I started working on the Dennis PD.

"Okay, son, just take it easy. Show me to the room."

Jim and I followed the officer through the living room and down a short hallway to the right that led to a master bedroom suite with a bathroom, obviously modified from the house's original design. It was lined in white breadboard, more than halfway up each wall, with pale blue painted sheetrock above. An all-glass shower stall was on the right and a large tub with whirlpool jets was at the far end of the room; a skylight brought daylight down onto the tub. A stereo system was built into the wall over the toilet. On the left side as you entered was a double sink vanity with brushed nickel faucets. I'm glad Natalie didn't see this. It might give her ideas.

A photographer was taking pictures as we entered. The products of his work today would probably be the most grisly of his life, pictures he would not soon forget.

An officer handed me a pair of rubber gloves and I slipped them on. I didn't want to touch anything, but you never know. Pearson did the same.

The room smelled of death, blood and vomit. I hadn't been in such a disgusting place in a long time. I'd seen some pretty horrible things in my days on the METs in Boston, cases with beheadings and dismemberment, but I'd never seen one that was abandoned by the killer in mid-act.

"The boyfriend threw up when he saw her," said the officer with the gloves, pointing to the floor. I danced around it.

The woman's body was sitting upright against the back of the tub, her head turned to her right. There was a small cut mark on the left side of her throat. The killer was probably about to behead his victim when he was interrupted by the boyfriend entering the house. Her feet, arms and legs were at the drain end of the tub, scattered like a fisherman tossing his catches onto a boat deck.

As I got closer, I noticed some blood on the back of her head. I bent down to get a better look and saw what appeared to be a trauma mark under the blood. I'd let the M.E. make a final determination, but my money was on death by blunt force trauma to the head. The killer must have snuck up on her and hit her hard with something solid. I looked around the floor, but found nothing.

I went back to the officer with the note pad at the front door. "Any sign of a weapon or weapons?"

"No, sir, we haven't found anything yet. The kitchen is undisturbed. The knives are all in place."

"Look for a pipe or a hammer, too. She was hit over the head with something hard." In cases like this, the killer usually cleans up thoroughly after the job, but because this one was interrupted, he might have gotten sloppy.

I took one more look in the bathroom, but didn't find anything else, so I was about to step out to let the photographer and the forensic techs do their thing. The M.E. came into the room and stopped short of the bathtub. "Oh, no. What in the world? I trust this woman was dead before he started cutting."

I spoke without looking at him. "That's what you're here for, Doc. There's a wound on the back of her head that might answer that question. Give her the full works, though, including a rape kit. You never know with these creeps."

The boyfriend wasn't in very good shape for talking, but I had no choice. I introduced myself and went through the usual battery of questions about possible enemies, unusual activities or interests, financial situation, etc. The couple had lived here for six years and had decided to get married. I guess they wanted to make sure before taking the big step. Things sure had changed in twenty-five years.

His name was Clifford Clarkson, thirty-six years old, although he looked younger, thin build and appeared to be about average height while sitting down. I could be wrong. He was a high school teacher at Dennis-Yarmouth Regional and operated a charter fishing boat out of Sesuit Harbor during the summer. He had no known enemies, didn't owe anybody money, other than the big boat loan, and got along well with all his neighbors.

Cases on the Cape were surely different from those in Boston, where I usually dealt with victims who were either criminals themselves or hung out with them; people who lived too close to the edge. Here, it seemed everybody loved everybody, or pretended to.

Mr. Clarkson agreed to move out for a few days and told me where he could be reached. I gave him my card and told him I'd be in touch, and checked with Jim Pearson out front. He already had officers canvassing the street.

"Geeze, Jack, another one in broad daylight," said Jim. "Somebody must have heard or seen something. Two murders and a B and E. Dennis PD hasn't been this busy in a long time. I'm not counting last year, because some of that stuff was off-Cape."

"The work still qualified for overtime, Jimbo, but I see what you mean. No FBI involvement this time, and I hope it stays that way."

Officer Orlando approached us and broke off our conversation. She spoke rapidly.

"There's a woman in that house across the street, next to the wooded lot, who wants to speak with you, Detective Contino. She said she saw somebody leave this house."

"Orlando, you're with me." I hustled my way across the street, but avoided running. I didn't want to draw unneeded attention. I knocked on the front door; it opened before I could deliver a second one.

"Hello, Ma'am, I'm Detective Jack Contino."

"Yes, I told the nice young lady there I wanted to talk to the man in charge." She glanced past me at Officer Orlando and gave her a slight smile. The woman was mid-forties, shoulder length black hair, wearing tight black Capri pants and a black sleeveless top, with a mock turtleneck. I guess black was her color.

She invited us in, gave me her name, Mrs. Gail Underhill, and began describing what she saw, without moving from the entryway. She had the odor of whiskey on her breath.

"A little while ago, I heard Blake arrive home and saw her go into the house. It was a half hour later, maybe longer, when I heard another car arrive. That was Cliff. I watched him walk up to the front door and try to open it, but it apparently was locked. He seemed frustrated or at least surprised by that, since nobody locks their door—while somebody's home, anyway. So he had to use his key to open the door. Just as he went in, I saw a man run out from behind the house. He came across the street and ran through that wooded lot next door to my house."

"Did you get a good look at him, Ma'am?"

"Yes, but not his face. I mean, he was kind of husky, had jeans on with sneakers and a sweatshirt, a hooded sweatshirt, you know, with the hood pulled up. I couldn't get a good look at his face."

I asked Officer Orlando to take notes as we talked. "Could you see his complexion, Ma'am?"

"Do you mean was he white or black? Oh, he was white, all right. So were his sneakers, come to think of it."

"So he ran through that lot. Could you see where he went from there?"

"No, sir, I didn't think to look out back. Then I heard Cliff screaming, so I stayed here, looking at his house. I was scared, you know. I had no idea what was going on, but that screaming got me scared. After a while, the police cars and a fire truck showed up. That really got me worried, so I poured myself a drink. Then there were more police cars. Funny, I was scared but, with all the police showing up, I started to feel better."

"Was there anything else, Ma'am?"

"No, it all happened so fast, you know, Cliff getting home just as that man ran out of his yard. The young lady officer there told me what it was, that a woman had been killed inside. I just can't believe it. Blake Hairston, poor girl. And Cliff. They were engaged, you know."

"Yes, we know. Thank you so much for your help, Ma'am. We may have to contact you later."

"Oh, I understand that, Detective. I watch those police shows on TV. Sometimes you have to just keep going back to the witnesses to talk. I really like the way Columbo does it. He fools those bad guys into thinking he's just a dim wit, but he's so smart. He always gets them."

I excused myself in polite policeman fashion and rushed to the next lot, motioning Officer Orlando to join me. The guy's trail could still be hot and I wanted to follow it myself. We looked for footprints or bushes that were stomped down, starting along the road edge. I didn't see anything, but Officer Orlando, about fifteen feet away from me, saw something and called out. "Detective, this might be something over here."

There were some weeds and crabgrass that got taller as we moved away from the edge of the road. A narrow path had been worn there by many years of people cutting through. It wove its way through the tall bushes and trees and I could make out the distinct sneaker tread from a recent trespasser.

The old pine trees got taller and thicker and some oaks that never got more than six to eight inches thick filled the lot. The scraggily pines had no bottom limbs, just bare trunks with thick bark. The branches were near the top, with long needles growing from the smallest twigs. Pine cones were scattered on the ground, many of them crushed under foot by human traffic.

The trail was easy to follow, so I picked up my pace. I could hear Karen Orlando, right behind me, seeming to nudge me on. She probably wanted to rush past me, but kept behind, like a good subordinate. I knew the killer was long gone, but I edged to the right of the path and waved her past me, like a driver motioning another one to pass. She hit a higher gear and pulled away from me.

She reached the opposite side of the lot where it opened onto another street, not a cul-de-sac, but a road that curved through the neighborhood. I caught up with her and we stopped there, looking in all directions: left, right, across the street and even back from where we came. Nothing.

Like most streets on the Cape, there was a sprinkling of sand along the road's edge and I peered at it for signs of tire marks. I found a clear footprint, left by his sneaker, but no tire marks. Karen moved down the road one way and I went another, then we turned and walked back toward each other. I walked across the street, thinking that he might have parked on the other side, but found nothing there, either.

There were houses up and down both sides of the street and all of them had paved driveways, clear of sand.

"What did he do, fly out of the neighborhood?" I groused to Orlando.

"Maybe, Detective, he parked in somebody's driveway, or he had someone waiting for him, an accomplice."

"Or he just kept running down the street, but I doubt it. He got to her house just after she arrived home, so he probably followed her. He had to be parked close by. Let's get Pearson and Davis and start knocking on doors. Somebody must have seen a car and Mr. Hoodie."

About forty-five minutes later, we had canvassed the street. Three of the houses near the vacant lot were summer rentals and were empty. Other houses with year-round owners saw nothing unusual. They were either in their kitchens, away from front windows, or were in bedrooms, or in basements or anyplace other than where they would see a stranger's car parked on the street. It was another dead end for us.

Officer Orlando stepped closer to me. She still held a notepad in one hand and she began tapping it with the other. "Detective, you said he must have been following her, probably from where she worked, at Cape Cod Community College. Maybe someone saw the guy there, without even knowing it."

"Good catch, Officer. Oh, and when are you going to stop calling me Detective? I'm Jack."

"Okay, Detective . . . Jack."

Chapter Eleven

We wrapped up our work at the crime scene and I drove home, taking Route 6-A. The slow pace along the meandering Old King's Highway, which passed through the north side of the Cape, was relaxing and therapeutic. The villages along this route had historic zoning, so it wasn't lined with motels, fried fish joints and miniature golf courses. Its leisurely pace was rarely the fastest way to get anywhere on the Cape, but that's why I liked it.

Nat was making a beef stew in a crockpot, perfect for this early fall evening, with cloudy sky and falling temperature. It was almost done by the time I got home. Nat was sitting in the living room, wearing a pair of black jogging pants and a red long-sleeved jersey with no marking on it. She was reading a magazine and greeted me with "Hi, Hon," without looking up.

I moved slowly toward her while slipping off my jacket and slinging it over one shoulder, kissed her on the cheek and went into the bedroom to change into jeans and a Kelley green jersey with the Celtic logo in front. Her voice broke through the air.

"I made an appointment for you at the doctor's office for that physical. He had a cancellation tomorrow morning, so I booked you. You have to fast after midnight so they can draw blood."

I closed my eyes when I heard her, hoping that I heard wrong. Of course, that didn't work, so I went back to the living room to face the music.

"Hon, I can't go tomorrow morning."

"Why not? You promised me that you would get that physical and you're going to keep that promise."

"Nat, I'm too busy right now. I just don't have the time."

Nat kept looking at the magazine, her resolve intact. "You never have the time. That's why you have to make the time. You know the old saying, if you want a job done, give it to a busy person. You're a busy person and you're going to get this job done."

"Nat, you don't understand. There was another murder today."

She finally put the magazine down and looked at me. "Oh, Jack. That's horrible, another murder?"

"Yes, a young woman, a teacher at four Cs. It was very brutal. The killer dismembered her in her bathtub."

Natalie got up from her chair and rushed to me, throwing her arms around my neck in a conciliatory hug. She didn't need to speak to make me feel better.

"I've got to go to the college first thing and talk to people over there. We believe the killer may have followed her from work, so maybe somebody saw him."

"How would they know?"

"They wouldn't, but we got a description from a neighbor who saw a man running from the victim's house. Maybe someone at the college saw the same guy. I sure hope so, because we've got to catch this guy soon."

Nat pulled back and gave me a puzzled look.

"Nat, this guy fits the same description as the other killer, and the one who broke into the liquor store. We thought the first one was an isolated case, somebody with an axe to grind against the victim, Robert Schroeder. Now, I don't know what's going on. We've got to find out if there's a connection. I have to go to the college first thing tomorrow."

Natalie sighed. "Of course you do, Jack, right after the physical. Good thing I scheduled it for eight o'clock."

I looked at her with my head tilted to one side, like my ears weren't working properly. "Nat, didn't you hear me? I've got to focus on this case. I can't take the time..."

"Oh, yes you can, and you will. A physical will only take about an hour and then you can get over to the college. You're not going to solve the case by nine anyway. You're good, Jack, but you're not that good. Nobody is. I won't take no for an answer on this."

"Nat..."

"Don't *Nat* me. Don't be a baby about this. I almost lost you to that bullet once. I'm not taking any chances, so just get it done tomorrow and then you'll have the rest of the day to chase this killer."

Women. Why do they have to be right so many times?

Calculation   Steven P. Marini

The nurse removed the electrodes from my body following the EKG and wiped the gooey stuff off my skin. Physicals always made me feel uncomfortable, more so as I got older. They were pretty simple in the old days, like the Army one. They listened to your heart and lungs, checked your privates and back door and looked at your feet. I never could figure that one out. What did they think an eighteen-year old would have on his feet?

Nowadays, they had all this electronic stuff. And there was a doo-dad that he used over each eye, checking for something he called glaucoma. I never heard of it, but I guess I didn't have it, so that was good. Then came the bad news.

"Jack, you're way past the age when you should have had your first colonoscopy. You really need one."

Dr. David King was a likable guy, mid-forties, kept in shape; Nat talked about him a lot.

"I'm not sure what that is, Doc, but I don't like the sound of it. I know what the colon is and it's not a part of me that I want to share with anybody. It sounds like a scope is involved, going like, what is it they say on that Star Trek show, where no man has gone before. The whole idea of the thing doesn't set well with me."

"Jack, it's a screening test for colon cancer, a major killer of men in this country. It's what got Vince Lombardi because he didn't get screened, even though he had symptoms. Hell he'd still be coaching today if he'd taken care of himself. You're still in your fifties, Jack, so you should have a lot of years left. Got any grandchildren yet?"

I stared at the Doc for a while, then turned my head.

"I can give you the name of a good gastroenterologist. He's right here in the building. We've got good specialists in this practice, Jack."

"Don't do me any favors, Doc. Look, I've got a lot on my plate right now. We've had two murders in Dennis recently, so I don't want to take time away from work."

"You won't miss more than a day of work. I'm sure you can manage that. It's an outpatient procedure, but you'll be sedated and someone will have to drive you home. Could your wife do that? We can do it on one of her off days."

Natalie was an RN and worked part time at Dr. King's practice in Hyannis.

"Yeah, sure, she'll be happy to do it."

"You know, Jack, women need this procedure, too. Why don't you get yours done and then Natalie can do it a week or so after you?"

A smile crept across my lips. I hope the Doc didn't notice. The remark about grandchildren echoed in my ears. Maybe we'd be grandparents one of these years.

"Okay, Doc, I'll see the guy on my way out."

"Good, Jack. I'll write up a referral for you. He'll book you for an introductory appointment and then schedule the procedure. Talk to Natalie about it tonight."

"Will do. Now, what about today? How's everything look?"

"I don't see any problems so far, Jack. Your old wounds don't seem to be having any complications. It's not unusual for some pain from that abdominal one. It's only a few years old, so that's fairly fresh, but it's not going to kill you. You came out on top of that one, Jack. Believe me, your colon health is a much more significant issue at your age. We'll have the results of your blood tests in about a week, two at the most. We'll give you a call. You're all done here today, Jack. Get dressed and go catch those killers. You know, Jack, I understand you've done a lot of that in your career. I'm glad we've got you on the Cape now."

"Thanks, Doc. I appreciate the vote of confidence."

Killers, he said. I guess I should be happy that it's probably only one.

Chapter Twelve

My physical was over by nine-fifteen, but it felt like it was past noon. And now I've got to go through this colonoscopy thing. I'd rather be chasing killers.

I headed out of the parking lot on West Main Street in Hyannis and drove west to the airport road, made a left and proceeded to the rotary that turned me onto Route 132. The route was much less busy than it had been just a month ago, when summer residents and tourists jammed the Cape. The ride to the four C's campus was a breeze.

I pulled into the campus entrance, followed the one-way drive until buildings emerged on the left. The driveway had a pull-off area to the left for drop-offs and pick-ups, so I swung into it and stopped. An elderly man in a guard uniform was standing a few feet away. Campus security was a serious position at major colleges. Some, like the ones at Tufts University near where I used to live, received their training at the State Police Academy. I got to know some of those boys when I was with the METs. At the community college, these men were retirees, trying to keep busy in their later years and earn an extra buck. I don't know if any of them had law enforcement backgrounds, but I respected them for putting on the uniform. It can become a target when seen by the wrong kind.

The guard watched me work myself out of my car and step up onto the curb.

"Good day, sir," he said. "Picking somebody up?"

"No, officer, I have other business." He seemed to straighten up when I called him officer, as if he didn't hear it in a respectful manner very often and was pleased. I motioned him close and pulled my badge wallet out of my sport coat pocket and showed it to him.

"Oh, hello Detective. Maybe I can help you."

"How do I get to the college president's office?"

"Why, it's right in that main building off to the left, on the second floor. Well, heck, let me take you there."

I nodded and let the guard enjoy his unexpected duty, following him. I stopped and looked back for a moment. "Oh, officer, is my car all right there?" I said, pointing to it.

"Yes, sir, it sure is. I'll take care of that."

He guided me to a door under a wooden sign—the kind you see on some people's houses on the Cape with their names engraved on it, reading BUILDING. Its blue background and white lettering contrasted with the red brick building. We entered a small lobby with a single elevator and he pushed the up button, summoning the lift. We took it to the second floor and entered a carpeted lobby, with chairs and two-seat sofas with wooden frames and arm rests. We turned left and approached a woman seated at a desk outside what appeared to be a large office.

"Good morning, Alice. Is Dr. Hunter in?" said the guard.

"Yes, but he's very busy right now. Is he expecting you?" she asked, looking at me, as if the guard wasn't there.

I turned to the guard and thanked him for his help while shaking his hand. "I can take it from here, officer."

"You bet, Detective. Glad to be of service. And your car will be just fine. I'll take care of that, like I said." He turned and left, with a new spring in his step.

"Detective?" she said. "Is there something I can help you with?"

"Yes, I need to see the president, Dr. Hunter."

"Is he expecting you? He's very busy right now," she said, repeating her lines, which I suspect she repeats dozens of times per day. The way she ignored the guard and the stuffiness of her tone put her on my shit list right away.

"Ma'am, I'm Detective Contino with the Dennis Police. A member of the faculty was murdered yesterday. I need to speak with the college president and the head of campus security, now."

With her eyes wide and her mouth open, she scrambled out of her chair and ran into the president's office. I could hear their voices and in a moment, they both emerged.

"Hello, Detective. I'm Dr. Hunter, James Hunter. Please come in."

Alice stood there gaping at us as he motioned me into his office and ordered her not to mention anything to anyone.

"Detective, did you say a member of our faculty was murdered? I can't believe it. Who was it? How did it happen?"

"Slow down, Dr. Hunter." I had dealings with academic types many times around Boston. Some were down-to-earth guys regardless of the degrees after their name. Some were pompous asses. I pegged this guy for the latter. Nonetheless, I wanted to avoid a pissing contest with this fellow, so I knew I'd get more from him if I showed respect.

"Before we get into it in detail, I'd like you to summon your head of campus security. That way, I can cover all this at once and you'll both get the same information at the same time. I hope he's available."

"I'll make sure he is, Detective. Our security comes under the Director of Facilities. That's Bob Anthony. His office is in the facilities building, just a short walk from here. I'll have Alice call him. Please have a seat. I'll be right back."

He stepped out of the room for a moment and I took a seat near the end of a conference table that was part of the office décor. As was my custom, I sat with my back toward the wall, giving me a full view of the room and the door. I would have expected him to have a separate conference room, but maybe Dr. Hunter was an introvert and liked to do most of his admin work right here. Or maybe he was just a control freak.

Dr. Hunter came back into the room and immediately took the seat at the head of the table, where I'm sure he usually sat when conducting meetings. "Bob will be here right away. I didn't tell him what happened, just that he needed to drop everything and get over here."

So far, the man showed good instincts about an emergency. Maybe it was fear, maybe it was smarts, whatever. At least he didn't panic. He sat straight in his chair, hands folded on the table. He had on a nice looking, dark blue suit with a red power tie and a white shirt with cuff links. There was a pin in his lapel that showed the seal of the Commonwealth of Massachusetts. I recalled that the community college system was run by the state and guessed that it was a years-in-service pin.

"Nice looking pin," I said.

"Thank you," he said, a tight smile creasing his face. "It represents twenty years in service with the Commonwealth."

"You've been here that long?"

"No, no, Detective, but I've been in the community college system that long. I've been here six years. Before that, I was the Dean of Administration at Northern Essex Community College in Haverhill. I've worked at two others, but I won't bore you with the details."

"No, no, not at all, Dr. Hunter."

"How about you, Detective? How long have you been a police officer on the Cape?"

I needed to kill some time until Bob Anthony arrived, but I didn't feel like going into my life history. I just gave him some quick background. "I've just been here a couple of years. We used to live in Somerville and I made a career with the Metropolitan District Commission Police."

"Yes, I'm familiar with the Commission. John Fleer, the former Commissioner, is an old friend. I know there was a police department within the Commission. They patrolled all the parks and MDC facilities. Is that what you did, Detective?"

I heard a slightly snobbish tone in his question, but maybe I was hearing wrong. I gave him the benefit of the doubt, this time.

"Early in my career, I was on patrol. But I moved up to detective eventually, and served as special liaison to the FBI."

"The FBI. What kind of work was that, if I may ask?"

"Mostly fighting organized crime, Doctor. Boston has its fair share, I'm sorry to say."

"That sounds quite dangerous, Detective, but you seem to have escaped unscathed."

"Escape is a good word."

"What made you come to Cape Cod?"

"Let's just say it was time for a change."

Dr. Hunter's face stiffened. Perhaps he was realizing that police work has its hazards and that in Boston, the Mob plays for keeps. I think he sensed that I had a bigger story than I wanted to talk about.

"Good morning, Dr. Hunter. What seems to be the trouble?" A man walked into the office and came straight to the table, looking me over as I stood up.

"Bob, this is Detective Contino from the Dennis Police. I'm afraid he has some serious news for us. Please sit down."

We shook hands and he introduced himself, before sitting in the chair opposite me. He was a short man, about forty-five years old and wore a brown double-knit leisure suit, yellow shirt and black tie. A set of keys jingled from his belt. I made an effort not to look at it.

I gave them the grisly details of the murder and watched their faces for reactions. Bob Anthony looked shocked and he swung his gaze back and forth from me to Dr. Hunter. He had no idea who the victim was, but I guess his work didn't bring him into much contact with the faculty.

Dr. Hunter went pale, but he went immediately into questioning mode. "Detective, are you suggesting that the killer was here on campus and followed Ms. Hairston home?"

"It looks that way. A witness said Ms. Hairston arrived, followed by her boyfriend about twenty to thirty minutes later. She saw a man running out from behind Ms. Hairston's house as the boyfriend entered the front. The killer came into the neighborhood on foot through a wooded lot, so he must have had a car himself, because he got away so quickly. He wasn't prowling the neighborhood. He must have stalked Ms. Hairston from somewhere and the logical starting point is here on campus. That's why I need to talk to her colleagues and any students who might have been near Ms. Hairston before she left."

"You don't think it was one of our students," said Dr. Hunter.

"I don't know. It could have been anybody, at this point. Someone could have been here, mixing in, but not a real student. I can't rule out anything yet. That's why I'm here, to find out as much as I can."

Bob Anthony still hadn't spoken. I guessed he was better at getting the lawns mowed than he was at security.

Dr. Hunter tapped his fingers on the table and bit his lip at the same time. "Detective, I might have to shut down the campus, perhaps for a day or two. I have to consider the safety of the students and employees."

"Please don't do that until I've had a chance to interview a number of people. I'd like to do that right away. I want to call for a couple of officers to meet me here to help out."

"How much time will you need?"

"Hard to say, but give me until two o'clock this afternoon, if you can."

Dr. Hunter grunted softly and placed a hand flat on the table.

"Look, Doctor, I understand your concern for your people and the students, but if you send everybody home now, I might lose a potential witness. We have a limited description of the killer, so maybe someone saw him on campus. We need to investigate that possibility."

"Yes, but if there's a killer around here, and such a demented one, at that..."

I didn't want to share more information with these two, but the doctor wasn't leaving me much choice. I couldn't let him shut the college down just yet.

"I'm going to tell you something that you must keep to yourselves."

Dr. Hunter sat forward in his chair and leaned on his arms at the table. Bob Anthony's demeanor didn't change.

"This is the second murder in recent days involving someone fitting the same description. The first one had no connection to the college that we know of. That's why I don't believe the killer is a further threat to the people on campus. It does mean that there is a dangerous person out there who needs to be stopped, so I need all the help I can get."

Bob Anthony finally spoke. "There was a story in the newspaper about a murder in Dennis at a condo. The guy owned a liquor store. Was that the one?"

I waited before answering. "Yes. I'm trying to keep the details close to the vest, so you cannot repeat this information to anyone. Please, give me the time I've asked for. I'll have my officers in plain clothes, but I'm sure the word will spread that cops are on campus and something big has happened. Once that word gets out, a lot of people will hit the road anyway, so you can lock it down then. What do you say?"

Bob Anthony spoke up again, as if this news had finally sunk in and he wanted to play cop. "I could call in the off duty security men and station them around campus."

"No, Mr. Anthony. Thank you, but that won't be needed," I said. *Heavens, no.*

Dr. Hunter sat back in his chair, stared at Bob Anthony and then at me. "Very well, Detective, I'll wait until you've conducted your investigation. Bob, don't alert any of your officers just yet. Let Detective Contino have some room. We don't want to put a scare into the whole campus. I'll tell Alice to keep the lid on it, too. What's next?"

"I need to use your phone to call headquarters, and I need to know where Ms. Hairston's office is. Then I want to start with her supervisor and colleagues."

"Very well, Detective. Let's get started."

Chapter Thirteen

I made a quick call to headquarters and spoke with Jim Pearson. I told him to get Officer Orlando and to report to me at the college in plain clothes. I'd be on the second floor of the North Building where Ms. Hairston's department chair had his office.

Dr. Hunter escorted me across the campus to North Building. Once on the second floor, he took me past a secretary's desk just outside a string of faculty offices.

"Hello, Phyllis. Is David in?" asked Dr. Hunter.

"Good morning, Dr. Hunter. Yes, he is." She was a woman in her mid-forties, with wire-rimmed glasses and a pleasant smile. She looked at me, as if expecting an introduction, but there was none.

A voice came from an office with the name David Millis, Department Chairman, posted on a plaque outside the door. "Don't tell me I'm in trouble again. Did I miss a faculty meeting or something?"

A young man, probably in his thirties, emerged from the office. He had short dark hair and wore a yellow shirt, blue tie and dark slacks, flared at the leg, a popular style. He stood just under six feet, by my guess, and was in good shape.

"Good morning, David," said Dr. Hunter. "Let's move into your office."

We stepped into the small office, and Dr. Hunter closed the door behind us. We remained standing for the introductions and Dr. Hunter prepared David for the shocker. "This is Detective Contino from the Dennis Police Department, David. I'm afraid he has some terrible news."

When I told David what had happened, he stood silent for a prolonged period, his jaw dropped. He clenched his right hand into a tight fist and pressed it into the palm of his left, twisting it slowly. He turned away from us for a moment, and then turned back.

"This is unbelievable. Blake. She was just here yesterday. I was talking to her, so was Linda, in her office next door. Damn. How can something like that happen? I mean, you read about things in the newspaper, but you never expect it to being so close, you know."

Dr. Hunter spoke. "Calm down, David. This is terrible. We're all shocked by it, that is, the few of us who know."

"Nobody else on the faculty knows?" said David.

"Not yet, David. You're her supervisor, so you needed to be told first. Here's what's going to happen. Detective Contino needs to conduct an investigation. He'll start by talking to you. He has officers coming over to talk to other faculty and students. At two o'clock this afternoon, I'm going to shut down the campus and call the faculty and staff into a meeting in the auditorium, where I'll make the announcement. Of course, many of you will know about it by then, but I want to get everybody together for a formal announcement. I'll excuse myself now, so I can go back to my office and prepare for the meeting. Detective, if you need me, feel free to call my office."

Dr. Hunter left the room and I heard the secretary wish him a good day, but there was no reply.

"David, what can you tell me about yesterday afternoon when you spoke to Ms. Hairston?"

"Well, she was in and out of her office, the one she shares with another part-time faculty member. I spoke with her briefly, nothing important, just small talk, you know. She was engaged to be married and I kidded her about that, just having fun."

"Why did you kid her about that?"

"She had been living with this guy for a long time, a few years, but they never tied the knot. Now, they finally decided to make the move, so I'd kid her about finally becoming an honest woman, you know, nothing big and she had a good sense of humor."

"Okay, what else?"

"Nothing, really. I didn't spend much time with her, actually. I was always just happy to see her in the office. She was quite nice to look at." There was a pause. "She was a damned good teacher, too. She was with Linda Pinkney mostly. She's the teacher who has the office next to mine. I think she was the last one to talk to her. She should be in her office now."

"Really. I'll talk to her next. Thanks, David. I'm real sorry to bring you such bad news today. I need a favor from you, David. I need a list of all her students for the past year and their grades."

"You think a student could do this over a bad grade?"

"I've seen lesser motives for murder. It's not likely, but I have to check it out."

"Yeah, sure, I can get that for you. I'll have the Registrar print it out right away."

"Thanks, and don't tell him what it's about. I need a little time before the news spreads across the whole campus."

"I understand, Detective."

"Thanks." I gave him my card and the usual request to call me if he thought of anything.

Linda Pinkney's door was open and she was sitting behind her desk, facing the door. Apparently full-timers didn't have to share an office, for it was the only desk there. I knocked on the open door as I walked in, stopping just over the threshold.

"Hello, Ms. Pinkney, I need to speak with you privately." I showed my badge before closing the door. She didn't seem startled. She must have heard me and Dr. Hunter arrive in the area, so she remained seated with her hands folded on the desk. "I'm Detective Contino with the Dennis Police. I have some very bad news for you and I need to ask you a few questions about this incident."

"It's *Mrs.* Pinkney, Detective." She waited for me to speak, no need to ask the obvious question.

Her hand went over her mouth when I told her the news; I left out the part about dismemberment. She started to cry, not a hard sobbing cry, but slow and soft, as if her tear ducts were opened just part way. I gave her time.

"Who could do such a thing?" she asked. "Why? Why?"

"That's what we intend to find out. Perhaps you can help me. I understand you may have been the last person to speak with her before she left the campus yesterday. What did you talk about?"

Mrs. Pinkney choked back her tears and sucked in a breath of air. "Well, let me see, we talked about her engagement, for one thing. She explained that after all their years together, they finally agreed that they'd like to have a family and they believed a marriage was the best way to raise a child. She thought time was getting short for her in terms of getting pregnant. Funny, when a woman turns thirty she thinks the world sees her as being over the hill. I don't think the men felt that way about her. She was very good looking with a great figure."

I looked at the chair against the wall. "Mind if I sit down for a minute?" Mrs. Pinkney nodded approval. I dragged the chair closer to her desk and slid into it. It felt good to take a load off my big feet. "What else did you talk about, Mrs. Pinkney? Did you discuss work at all?"

"She said she had a couple of really good students this semester, in different classes. She had two sections of English Composition. One boy and one girl. They worked hard and wrote very well. She thought they both belonged in a four-year college, but I guess finances sent them here first."

"Was there anyone causing her trouble?"

"No, I don't think so, at least she didn't mention that."

"So, there wasn't anybody harassing her about a bad grade?"

"Like I said, I don't know of any such thing."

"What about anything sexual? Sometimes male students get the hots for a good-looking female teacher. Was there anything like that?"

"Oh, sure, there's always somebody like that. I've had my share. We'd compare notes on that sometimes and have a good laugh. But I don't think she was having any serious problems with anyone."

"So it looks like nothing unusual was going on in her life or in her classes. It was just business as usual yesterday."

"That's about right, Detective."

"Was there any sign of someone stalking her? Did you notice anyone?"

"No, I can't say that I did."

"Okay, Mrs. Pinkney, that's all for now." I gave her my card. "I'd like to talk to your office secretary, if I could."

The investigation was off to a very slow start. Blake Hairston was a beautiful young woman, in a good relationship, everybody liked her, nobody was bothering her, nobody was stalking her—until her killer.

Calculation   Steven P. Marini

Mrs. Pinkney took me out to where the secretary, Phyllis Court, sat, and made the introductions, then excused herself. Of course, she was hurt and shocked to hear about Blake Hairston. I gave her plenty of time to compose herself before asking some questions. I asked her to recall the moments when Blake was in the building and getting ready to leave.

Mrs. Court had a ringside seat for most of the entire floor. There were chairs and sofas scattered about in the central area, with the offices along the perimeter on both sides. The furniture was in different arrangements throughout to break up the monotony of a long, straight, wide-open area. When I asked her if she saw anyone or anything unusual yesterday, I finally got a break.

"Yes, there was someone who bothered me."

"How so, Mrs. Court?"

"Well, there was this big guy, wandering around for a while. I didn't recognize him at all, so I didn't think he was a student. After a few weeks of a semester, you get used to the same faces in the building. He was new to me. He walked around for a time and then sat in a chair over there." She pointed to it. "He seemed to be checking out the area and he looked over this way a lot."

"What did he look like, Mrs. Court?"

"Like I said, he was big. Not as big as you. He looked too old to be a student, but you never know at a community college. He had on jeans and a dark sweatshirt with a hood. I remember that because at one point, he pulled the hood up over his head. I think he had brown hair and I didn't really see his eyes. You know, now that I think of it, he left just after Blake did. Oh, my God, do you think he was the . . . ?"

Mrs. Court began to tremble and tears filled her eyes.

I tried to calm her down. "I don't know, Mrs. Court. It may be nothing." Then I heard a voice call me.

"Here, Jack."

I looked up to see Officers Pearson and Orlando approaching in plain clothes, as instructed. Orlando's idea of plain clothes included tight jeans and a sweater, definitely not a cop look. Some of the male students noticed her easily. I briefed them on what I had learned so far and was about to have them check around for anybody who saw Mr. Hoodie. I kept quiet about Blake Hairston.

Phyllis Court had gotten the best look at the guy so far, so I asked her to come with me to headquarters to work with a sketch artist. Then I remembered that the guy we often hired for sketching worked here at the college in the Art Department. She called his office and asked him to come over right away. Maybe she could give the artist a good enough description to work up a decent sketch of the son-of-a-bitch.

I took Pearson and Orlando over to the cafeteria to kill time over coffee, while the artist worked with Phyllis Court. It was in the same building as the administrative offices, just across the quad. There were a few students and some faculty scattered around the room. Except for some stares at Officer Orlando, nobody paid attention to us, so perhaps the plain clothes strategy was working after all. I'm sure Pearson and I didn't look very interesting.

We bought our coffee and I couldn't resist a cheese Danish to go with it. Pearson and Orlando just had coffee. Pearson sneered at the Danish and broke into a grin. "That stuff will kill you, Jack."

"Hey, after a couple of decades in Boston and a bullet hole or two, I think a few extra calories won't hurt me. Besides, my weight is actually down a little."

"Really?"

"Yeah, about two pounds."

It was time to change the subject. "Let's focus on the job, folks. It looks like Mr. Hoodie was definitely here on campus yesterday and was watching Blake Hairston. Mrs. Court ID'd him and said he left the area when the victim did. No question he stalked her and followed her home."

"What more do we need to do on campus, Jack?" asked Orlando.

"We still need to talk to people to see if there is anything else we can get that adds to the description and we need to find out if anybody saw him in his car. A description of his vehicle could help a lot. A plate number would be great, but that's more than I'd expect."

"Got you," said Orlando. "We can canvas the parking lot and talk to people there."

Calculation   Steven P. Marini

"It's really strange, Jack," said Pearson. "We've got two murders, possibly by the same guy, but the methods are totally different."

I sipped my coffee, washing down a sizeable bite of my Danish. "It is pretty strange. One murder is like a gangland execution and the other looks like the work of a serial killer, a brutal and perverted serial killer. And don't forget the liquor store robbery. Seems like he threw that in just to add pain to the first victim's widow. But each witness describes this husky guy in jeans and a hooded sweatshirt."

"Did you ever have such a set of coincidences in Boston, Jack?" asked Pearson.

"No, I can't say we did. We had plenty of gang executions and a few ritualistic killings, really bizarre stuff. And, of course, there was the Boston Strangler. Our case looks like all the crimes were done by one guy, but with different MOs. That was definitely not the case in Boston. We had plenty of killers to go around. You might say they were specialists."

"That's the kind of specialist we can do without," said Orlando. She spoke without looking up.

"It's okay, Karen," I said. "We put Sidney Fish away." Fish is a killer we put away a year ago. "Paid killers are few on the Cape. Whatever this guy is, we'll get him, too. Let's go see if that sketch is ready."

I said goodbye to my cheese Danish with a final bite and gulped down the last of my coffee. In a minute, we were back at Phyllis Court's desk.

"Here you are, Detective." Mrs. Court held up the black and white sketch on a pad of paper. She also had several photo copies, which she handed to me, along with the original. There were two images on the pad, one above the other. The top image was a head and shoulders shot of the guy, three-quarter side view. The eyebrows were light and the cheeks were puffy and he had some circles under each eye. The bottom image was a long shot, showing the man sitting on the forward edge of a chair, his hands in the pockets of the sweatshirt.

"That's pretty good detail, Mrs. Court," I said.

"Well, the more Joe asked me about his features, the more I was able to remember. He's really good to work with."

Calculation   Steven P. Marini

I remembered him now. Joe Coburn was the name of the sketch artist. "Where is he now?"

"Oh, he's been gone quite a while now. It didn't take him very long. Do you want me to call him?"

"No, I'll thank him later, and pay him for his time, too."

I thanked Mrs. Court for her help and turned to my colleagues. "Let's get to work. Karen, Jim, go out into the student parking lot and ask anybody you see if they recognize this guy. Students come and go, so be prepared to hang out there for an hour or so. I'm going to show this to the college president and his Security Chief. After his faculty meeting, I'll have the Security guy post copies of this sketch around campus with our phone number on it. Maybe somebody knows him. I'll check back with you later. Good fishing."

I gave a copy to my colleagues and kept the original. We all stared at the images, as if we were making mental copies. The killer started to look real to me. Now we had a concrete image of the guy, not just whatever our imaginations dictated.

Chapter Fourteen

It wasn't the main headline in the local daily newspaper. The murder of a woman teacher at Cape Cod Community College was well down the front page, with the story continuing on page three. There were no pictures and no mention of dismemberment. *Chicken shit newspapers. Too gory for them to write the truth.*

He read the brief story again, as if his eyes deceived him the first time. He repeated the final sentence to himself. "Police are conducting a full-scale investigation." *No shit, Sherlock. What are they going to do, conduct a half-scale investigation?*

He poured himself another cup of coffee and sat down at the small kitchen table in his messy apartment. It was a small, one bedroom flat with a corner that passed for a kitchen, fully equipped with a twelve year old fridge, an electric range with an oven and a table with two dark wooden chairs. The living room was furnished with a sofa, brown vinyl, and a not so easy chair, upholstered in fabric. A fifteen inch TV, set on a shelf across from the furniture, completed the décor.

What's going on here? Another murder on Cape Cod, a freakin' homicide, and it isn't top news in this quiet little place? What are they up to? Or are they just plain stupid? Are the cops telling the newspaper to keep a lid on things? Well, whatever it is, I'm going to blow that lid sky high. They won't be able to ignore me much longer.

He sipped his black coffee, and flipped through the rest of the paper.

Nothing like caffeine to get my juices going. Helps me plan the action.

Oh, look at this. A prominent businessman pulled over for drunk driving, again. Mr. Grant Bartlett, part owner of the bankrupt Cape Cod Arena, couldn't hold his liquor. He got pulled over on West Main Street after a cop saw his car taking sharp curves on a straight road. You should never drink and drive, Mr. Bigshot Bartlett. Never drink and drive. Big shot owned part of a sports building. That reminds me of something.

He drank more coffee and began tapping his right index finger on the table.

The Cape Cod Arena was built with Mob money. Everybody knew that. This guy Bartlett was one of the owners, which means he must have owed the Mob guys some serious cash. He must be having trouble paying them back and so he drinks a wee bit to ease his tension. I think they call it something else now, since the Arena went bankrupt as a business. So now it's some kind of a warehouse or something, but it can't pay too well. I'll bet the Mob guys have Bartlett on their list. This just might work really well. Maybe I need to get a little closer to Mr. Bartlett.

He finished his caffeine fix, left the apartment and hopped into his worn down, dark gray Chevy. The engine was slow to start, so he slapped the dashboard in anger. *Shitbox, damn it.* He pumped the gas pedal a few times and tried the ignition again. *Success.*

The old concrete building was on White's Path in Yarmouth, a short drive out of Hyannis. It helped to know the back roads so he could avoid much of Rte. 28. Even during the off season it could be a pain. He parked near a side door located near a row of industrial type garage doors with loading docks, part of the renovation that took place after the Arena closed.

There was no lobby inside, just a small office area closed off from the warehouse. There was a window with an open part at the bottom, so people could talk and slide paperwork underneath. Nobody was inside, so he pulled up the hood to his sweatshirt, drew it tight on his head, and walked down an aisle with more offices. The office doors were closed, but they each had a window on them. He saw a name plate tacked on the wall beside each door. The first one said Grant Bartlett.

Looking inside, he saw Bartlett sitting at a desk, his necktie loosened and his collar open. He had a white shirt under a blue vest. His hair was graying on the sides. *I think you're going to do just fine, Mr. Bartlett. Yes sir, you'll do just fine.*

He was startled by the tap on his shoulder and it left him frozen for an instant. A deep voice broke through. "Can I help you?"

He turned around slowly and saw a shorter man, powerfully built, like he could lift a car without a jack. He had on gray work pants and a white sleeveless T-shirt, exposing massive arms that were deeply tanned. A small tattoo with an emblem he didn't recognize highlighted the man's right arm.

"Ah, no, I was just going to talk to Mr. Bartlett, but I can see he's pretty busy now. I'll come back later. It isn't important." He brushed by the muscular man, quick-stepping his way out of the building. The worker looked at the strange fellow in the hooded sweatshirt, thinking he was some kind of weirdo, but said nothing, looked through Mr. Bartlett's window, saw him on the phone and shrugged.

He looked straight ahead all the way to his car, got in and drove away. *Well, that was exciting. Wonder if little Hercules there is Bartlett's bodyguard. Maybe just a warehouse monkey. Here's a banana, Herc, go swing in some trees for a while 'til I need you.*

He drove east on White's Path, eyeing all the businesses that had popped up along the old road. *This place is getting crowded. Good thing I'm doing my part to check the population growth.*

He motored to North Main Street and headed south toward Rte. 28, crossed the Bass River Bridge into West Dennis and navigated to West Dennis Beach. The big parking lot had a couple of cars in it. He pulled up to the short wall that bordered the sandy beach, rolled his window down and sat there, taking in the calm waters and brisk breeze.

This is the Cape I like, the off season and not many people. Of course, the babes in bikinis during the summer are kind of fun to watch. I bet that school teach looked great in a bikini. What the hell, she looked great out of a bikini. Too bad I didn't get more time with that bitch.

The car door squeaked as he opened it, swung his chunky torso around, and pulled himself out. A couple of deep breaths felt good. He peered right, examining the expanse of beach. Then he swung his head left, noticing the old wooden bathhouse with its weathered shingles and dark roof, dotted with seagull droppings. He labored his way over the short wall and strode across the sand, hands in his pockets, reaching a spot behind the bathhouse. There were only a few feet of dry sand before it dropped off a bit, revealing dark, wet sand that marked the low tide area. He checked his watch and a grin creased his face. *This could be good. It just might do. No rush, though. I think I'll give Mr. Bartlett a little more time.*

Chapter Fifteen

Back in the president's office, I showed the sketch to Dr. Hunter and Bob Anthony. "This fellow looks a little older than our students, but it's hard to tell," said Dr. Hunter. "A lot of people dress like that, even some of the staff, but not the faculty. I still believe that teachers need to show some professionalism and dress the part. There needs to be some distance between faculty and students."

Hearing Dr. Hunter, Bob Anthony looked down for a moment and made a face. "It's not unusual for the grounds keepers to wear jeans and sweatshirts on cold days, but this guy doesn't look like any of my men, thank goodness. They're all good guys—good, hard-working men who do an important job keeping the campus infrastructure intact."

"Of course they do, Bob," said Dr. Hunter. "I'm quite proud of the way they maintain this campus. It's as good, if not better, than any other in the community college system. Yes, the faculty . . . and staff here are top notch."

It's always fun to watch people get caught in a pissing contest. "Please have some copies run off with our phone number on it and post them around campus after your meeting." I jotted down the headquarters number and gave it to Bob.

"I've been thinking, Detective," said Dr. Hunter. "It might be helpful if you attended the meeting, too. Your presence might encourage people to get involved if they know anything."

The request caught me off guard, but it made sense. "Sure, I can do that. I have to get back to the office for a while, but I can be here in time for your meeting. Two o'clock, right?"

"Yes, the auditorium is in the Arts building. Meet me there. I'll speak to the people, tell them what's happened, and introduce you. Perhaps you can answer some questions. I'm sure they'll have some."

Calculation   Steven P. Marini

"I'll do what I can, Dr. Hunter, but you have to understand that this is an ongoing investigation, so I'm limited as to what information I can give out."

"Yes, of course, I understand that, Detective. Two o'clock, then."

I nodded and turned away.

I was getting hungry and since home was between the campus and the Dennis PD headquarters, I decided to swing by the house to grab a bite. Nat was working today, too bad. A sweet smile from her would have been nice, with the way I was feeling. Natalie was the true constant in my life. No matter how unpleasant work might be on any given day, she always brought my spirits up. She was the proof that there was order and goodness in the universe. So what if a few Klingons showed up now and then?

After downing a piece of leftover meatloaf from the fridge, I heated up some water for a quick cup of instant decaf. Amazing how I managed to get used to this stuff. Nat and my doc both urged me to make the switch, figuring my system didn't need any extra stimulation at my age.

I decided to call my old friend and ex-partner at the METs, Leo Barbado. I still relied on him to help me by sniffing out information and tracking down bad guys. He was a guy who got results then and now. He'd probably be at his Barbado Investigations office, the home of the detective agency he established after retiring from the METs.

His phone rang about four times before he picked it up. "Hello, Barbado Investigations, Barbado speaking."

"Glad to know you're still working. Another ring and I'd figure you're on the throne and I'd hang up. Hope you're still keeping the city safe."

"Well, if it isn't the oldest, fattest lifeguard on Cape Cod. How goes it, Detective?"

We exchanged a few more pleasantries, as always, and I brought him up to speed about my latest cases. The tone of conversation changed when I told him about Blake Hairston.

"What a sick bastard. Dismemberment. Geeze, I wish I could say we never heard of that kind of thing before. Reminds me of that one we had a couple of years ago. You got a tip about where some body parts could be found near Revere Beach. Found everything but the head. The snitch said it was the work of Sal DiFino, aka Sammy White. Never could make an ID or prosecute anybody. So, what do you think, is this guy a solo player or connected?"

"Hard to tell so far. His first kill has all the markings of a Mob job, but Blake Hairston, that's more like a deranged son-of-a-bitch getting his jollies. Either way, I'm going to find him."

"Well, you've had experience with both types, Jack, so it's not exactly new territory for you, I'm sorry to say. I'll do some checking around up here to see if there is any talk about your killer. Keep me posted on this. I'll do whatever I can to help."

"That's why I called. I figured I could count on you to do some sniffing around. You're still my favorite bad guy chaser. Your number is at the top of my phone list."

"Ain't I the lucky one? Hey, give my best to Nat. I'll try to get down there to see you soon. I could use a good meal."

"Got it, Leo. Talk to you later."

Leo had an ace up his sleeve—me. Nat suggested once that Leo should join me on the Cape. I'd leave the Dennis PD and we'd work Barbado Investigations together. It would be a much slower pace than in Somerville. There were no Winter Hill boys on the Cape. Hope that didn't change.

I decided there wasn't time to go back to HQ, so I went back to the college at the agreed-upon time and did my thing for the faculty and staff. Dr. Hunter made the announcement about Blake Hairston and the collective shockwave went around the room like there had been a nuclear blast. First, there was stunned silence, then the rumble of voices growing louder. I figured the word would have spread around the campus by now, but I guess I was wrong. We had kept the lid on it pretty good.

Dr. Hunter waved at the crowd with both palms pushing downward, asking for quiet. After he introduced me, I told the audience what I could, including the fact that there had been a previous murder, unrelated to Blake Hairston's, except that we had reason to believe that it might be the work of the same man. I braced myself for the Q and A.

A tall, athletic-looking young man stood up in the front row. "Detective, how many men are working on this with you?" He looked side to side at his peers, seeking their approval for what he thought was a tough question.

"We have the full resources of the department on this case, I assure you." I didn't break eye contact with him.

The same man spoke again. "Blake was well known and liked here, Detective. You've got to catch this guy." He made a fist with one hand and ground it into the palm of the other, like he was getting ready for a fight.

"And we will. As I said earlier, this man might have committed a previous murder. That victim had a wife and child. They deserve full attention, too."

The crowd rumble softened. The young man looked mollified and lowered himself into his chair, relaxing his hands.

A woman stood up in the middle of the room on the center aisle. "Detective, there are a lot of intelligent and talented people in this room who can help. Just tell us what we can do."

Sometimes police work is full of irony. We want the public to help whenever possible. On the other hand, we don't want a vigilante group rising up, pitchforks and torches in hand, rushing to kill the mad man's monster.

"Right now, you need to go about your work as usual. Remember your mission, which is to educate these young people. But go about it with one eye alert to anything out of the ordinary." This was the right time to hold up the sketch. "We're going to make copies of this sketch and distribute them. He was on campus the day Ms. Hairston was killed and he may have followed her after work. If anyone recognizes this man, please come forward. Call the Dennis Police. Our phone number will be on the sketch. If you see him, call us. Do not, I repeat, *do not* try to confront him. He may be armed and very dangerous."

Dr. Hunter broke in and reinforced my words to the employees. He also announced that the campus was closed for the rest of the day, but classes would resume the following day. On the day of Ms. Blake's funeral, the campus would be closed again. He thanked me for my help and promised the full cooperation of his people.

Classes as usual tomorrow. Sure. I remembered talking to my kids after President Kennedy was killed. They went back to school, but even in their elementary school, all anybody could talk about was the assassination. You have to try to move on, to get back to your normal life, but it's never as easy as that.

Chapter Sixteen

A week went by and we were still short on information that could help us, about either case. Pearson and Orlando scrounged up conflicting information about what might be Mr. Hoodie's car. One student said he saw the guy in the parking lot, getting into a beat-up Dodge Dart, brown maybe, and dents on the passenger side. Of course, he didn't have the plate number. A report from a faculty member said he saw the guy in the sketch leaning on a gray Chevy Nova, the paint worn away so that it looked like primer paint. There might be a hundred heavy-set guys wearing hooded sweatshirts on campus this year.

Jim and Karen visited the campus every day that week, looking for those cars. One day, they thought they'd caught a break. Jim spotted a Dodge Dart fitting the description we had. It was dented on the passenger side and was a light brown color. He waited for nearly two hours for the owner to show up. His patience was rewarded.

Jim, wearing plain clothes, approached the owner, clad in a dark hoodie and jeans. The only problem was that the guy wasn't a guy. It was a girl, about five feet, eight inches tall, and a bit on the pudgy side. The kid was scared sick to have a cop talking to her. Jim said she had a very high-pitched voice and her face began to sweat when they talked. He told her she wasn't in any trouble and that he was just doing his job and that he needed to check out the car. She let him look inside, including the trunk and he took the plate number and registration. Her license was valid. Jim said that if this kid was a vicious murderer, so was the Tooth Fairy.

There was never any sign of the gray Nova, which meant that was probably a better lead. The only problem was that now it would be a lot harder to find, since it wasn't likely to show up again on the campus. We put the word out to all the other Cape Cod police departments and the State Police to keep a watch out for this one.

This job in Dennis was supposed to be an easy one compared to working against the Mob in Boston. I grant you that the pace was a lot slower, generally speaking. But on the Cape, I didn't have a network of snitches and undercover moles to help me out. I didn't have scared punks who'd rat out their mothers to keep from going to prison. I didn't have newspaper and TV reporters doing their own investigative work. That could be a blessing sometimes and a big pain in the ass at others. The Boston media hadn't paid any attention to these two killings yet. Not yet.

Chapter Seventeen

We all have our morning routines before going to work; shave, shower, breakfast, get dressed. I was at the breakfast part, my favorite, scrambling some eggs and sniffing the bacon strips sizzling in the pan. But magic moments never last. Phone calls at home in the early hours are rarely social.

I downed a gulp of French Vanilla coffee, a wakeup call to my vocal cords. "Hello."

"We got a new one for you, Jack." The night watch commander had a voice like a fog horn.

"Wonderful. I was just cooking breakfast. Okay, give me the basics."

"Some guys fishing from shore at West Dennis beach caught a big one near the bathhouse, only it wasn't a fish. They snagged a body in shallow water. He's a white male in a business suit and he's sporting a couple of bullet holes in his back."

"Damn it. Life's getting complicated on old Cape Cod. Contact Jim Pearson and Karen Orlando and have them meet me there. I'm on my way."

"Don't worry, Jack. He's not going anywhere. Finish your breakfast. The M.E. is on his way, too."

I finished cooking the eggs and bacon, dumped them into a plastic box with a lid, poured my coffee into a travel mug and grabbed my car keys off a hook near the kitchen phone. Nat appeared just in time to give her a wave. Hands on hips, she gave me a look.

I got into my car and put my package on the passenger seat. Funny thing about plastic. I hear we're using too much of the stuff and it stays in the landfills forever. Maybe it's bad for us. But it saved my bacon and eggs today. I guess there's a time and place for most everything. I cranked up the engine, backed out of the driveway and headed for the beach.

I navigated some back roads to West Dennis beach, passed the Sand Dune nightclub on Lighthouse road and pulled up to the ambulance at the bathhouse. Pearson and Orlando were already there.

"Morning, Jack," said Jim. "I talked to the fishermen. They're sitting on the fence, over there." Jim pointed to a low fence that separates the parking lot from the sand. "They snagged their catch about forty-five minutes ago, just about sun up. There was nobody else around, as far as they could see. You want to talk to them?"

"Did you give them a card?"

"Yep."

"No, you can cut them loose. We can always get back to them."

"Yeah, I got their names and numbers, etc."

"Good, Jim. Let's talk to the M.E."

"Already did." It was Karen Orlando. "The guy took two bullets in the middle of the back from close range. He wasn't in the water very long, so he must have been dumped just before daylight. He'll do an autopsy right away and give you the official cause of death."

"Do we have an ID on the victim?"

Orlando flipped open her notepad. "Yes, he's Grant Bartlett, fifty-two years old, lives in Hyannis, according to his driver's license."

Jim Pearson nodded. "I know this guy, not personally, that is. He was part owner of the Cape Cod Arena. It went bankrupt and the facility was changed into a warehouse. I guess they lease space to other businesses. There was talk that he got mixed up with some bad people. Rumor has it that the financing for the Arena came from less than reputable lenders."

"I heard that, too, Jim. Maybe he still owed those guys a lot of money. Maybe those guys are from off Cape. I'll check with the State Police and the FBI. Orlando, see if he's got any family or an ex, and get to them before the local news people get on it."

She tucked away her notepad and scurried to her car. Jim and I looked at the victim being loaded into the ambulance and heard Orlando's car start up at the same time.

"Is the Light Tower Inn still open?" I asked. The Inn was a short distance away across the road. It was an old Cape landmark. I wasn't sure when it closed for the winter.

"No. It closed up two weeks ago."

"So I guess nobody would have been there to hear gunshots. Call the owners anyway, Jim, and check it out." There were no other buildings nearby except the Sand Dune. I told Pearson to check that one, too. I didn't think the shooting took place at the beach, but there was a chance.

It was full daylight, so I decided to walk around the area and take a close look. I wasn't sure of what I was looking for. Sometimes you just go through the motions. A detective's got to be detecting. I didn't find anything useful.

The rumble in my midsection reminded me that I still had some breakfast waiting for me. I drove to HQ and brought my culinary delight into the office and shoved it into the microwave oven for a minute. The night shift guys left a half pot of regular coffee, now smelling like old tires, so I decided to take the time to make some decaf. Some plastic forks were in a drawer under the coffee pot. I helped myself to a fork and waited for the coffee. The eggs and bacon tasted pretty good for their age. Those microwave ovens were a good deal.

What was going on here on old Cape Cod? I had three murders in less than a month. You'd think I was back in Boston dealing with the Mob. I wasn't sure what I was dealing with now. Robert Schroeder's killing looked like a professional hit, but Blake Hairston's case looked more like the work of a psycho, except that it sounded a little like the case Leo talked about over the phone. Sal DiFino was a strongman for Tommy Shea, leader of the Winter Hill boys. DiFino was currently in jail, but Shea was on the streets. He always managed to slip out of any nooses hanging close by.

Rumor had it that the now defunct Cape Cod Arena had been financed with Mob money. I heard that years ago, but I was with the METs back then and it was out of my jurisdiction, so I never got into it. I guess I needed to track down that rumor.

Jim Pearson came into the office in uniform, having finished checking for witnesses at the Light Tower and the Sand Dune. He found the manager of the Light Tower in his office, but he hadn't seen or heard anything. Nobody was home at the Sand Dune.

"Jim, I think a trip to the Registry of Deeds is in order. I want to find out more about the ownership of the Arena."

"Want me to come along?"

Looking through the land records is a one man job. "No. Wait here for Orlando. Check back at the Community College and with Anne Schroeder, just to see if anything new has come up and to let them know we haven't abandoned them. I'll meet back with the two of you later."

It was too early for the Registry of Deeds office to open, so I had another cup of decaf and grabbed the daily newspaper that was folded up next to the coffee pot. It was yesterday's paper, but I read it anyway. What the heck.

Searching for public records in Boston can be a full day's work and a considerable pain. Just getting around in the city was bad enough, although I had done it for years. On Cape Cod, a short drive into Barnstable Village on Rte. 6-A was like a stroll in the park.

The Registry of Deeds was in a small building adjacent to the Court House, and parking was not a problem that early. The inside of the building was dimly lit and had a lot of paneling and molding that made me feel like I was living in colonial times. A white-haired lady, about mid-fifties, helped guide me through my search and I was out of there in less than an hour.

I drove back to HQ and called Leo. The Cape Cod Arena was built on a large strip of land owned by Jonathan R. Winston and family. They leased the land to a corporation headed up by Grant Bartlett, Joshua Owings and Richard Browning. They built the Arena and a lien was held on the building by a firm called Back Bay Resources, Inc. That's a new one to me, so I decided to ask Leo to look into it for me.

As usual, it took about five rings for Leo to answer. "Leo, I said I'd call you back if I needed anything, so here I am again."

"Boy, two calls in about a week. Am I ever the charmed one. What's up?"

"I need to find out about a finance company called Back Bay Resources: who are they, who owns and runs it, do they specialize in any way with a certain clientele, that sort of thing."

"I gather you're not buying property, so this must be part of your murder investigations. Boy, it's good to know you're keeping busy."

"You don't know how busy, pal. We got another one last night. Some shore fishermen snagged a body off West Dennis beach. This one looks like a possible Mob hit."

I told Leo about Bartlett and his shaky business history at the Cape Cod Arena.

"Looks like you didn't move far enough away to find total peace and quiet. People are going to wonder about you and your serene little town. Back Bay Resources, eh? I'll get right on it."

"Thanks, Leo. What's new up there?"

"Barbado Investigations is doing great. We've got a couple of runaway wives we're chasing down, a cheating husband we're following, hoping to catch him in the act, and a fifteen year old who left home and the parents are afraid he's getting mixed up in some shenanigans at Suffolk Downs. It's all helping finance college funds for my State trooper friends working part time here."

"You see, Leo, if there weren't a lot of trouble in people's lives, we'd be on the street looking for a hand out."

"Yeah, thank goodness for social disharmony."

An hour after my call, Pearson and Orlando came in and I brought them up to speed. I had another visitor this morning, a reporter for the local newspaper. Her name was Lynn Bradford, a woman in her mid-forties, born and raised on Cape Cod. I met her early after my arrival in Dennis and we hadn't had any problems. She was good at her job, but she wasn't like some big city investigative reporters: aggressive and demanding. The Cape was her home and she wanted to serve the community well. Bringing important news to her readers was her aim.

Pearson handled the interview with Lynn Bradford, but she insisted on talking to me, too. She was going to be assertive this time.

"Good morning, Detective. Thanks for seeing me." She was tall, about five feet, eight inches, with short blonde hair and a trim figure, concealed at a professional level by a blue pants suit. She wore the jacket unbuttoned, revealing a white blouse. A large black purse was slung over one shoulder.

"Hello, Lynn. Nice to see you again. How can I help you?"

"I got the surprise over my scanner radio this morning and I'd have seen you earlier, but I've still got two kids to get ready for school. So I wanted to talk to you about it."

"I'm sure Pearson gave you the details."

"Yes, Jim is always cooperative with the press. But with three homicides over a very short time, Jack, I've got to find out what's going on. This is my home and I care a great deal about it."

"I appreciate that, Lynn. I really do. I used to live in Somerville and a lot of bad stuff happened there because of some locals who thought they were above the law. I raised kids, too."

She held a small pad and pen in her hand, waiting for me to give her something newsworthy, beyond the who, what, where, when and how that she got from Jim . She was poised, though, as if her posture was sufficient notice that I was expected to tell her something important to the community.

"Jack, do you have any leads, anything at all?"

"If you mean do we have any suspects, the answer is no. We've checked out people close to the first two victims and we haven't seen a motive attached to them. The murders were done differently, so there's no pattern there."

She jotted down some notes as I spoke. "What about this morning? Jim said it was a gunshot wound, two bullets."

"That's right, but it's too early to know anything more about Mr. Bartlett's murder."

"You don't have any witnesses?"

"Not eye witnesses, if that's what you mean. We did learn about somebody fleeing Blake Hairston's house and got a vague description. There was somebody seen at the college near her office who fits the description; his size, build and what he was wearing and some facial features. But the guy wore a hooded sweatshirt pulled tight on his head. We made a composite drawing and spread it around the campus."

"Can I have a copy?"

"Yes, of course." There wasn't much point in denying her information about Mr. Hoodie and the drawing, since

it was already in public view at the college, so I gave her a copy and a request. "Lynn, I'm going to ask a big favor. Please don't print the composite."

She dropped her arms to her sides and straightened up. "Why not, Jack? It might help you. Somebody might come forward if they think they know him."

"Yes, and it could spook the killer, too. The less he thinks we know about him, the better."

She took a deep breath while considering my request and released it in a sigh. "It doesn't seem right, Jack, but I'll honor your request, for now."

"Thanks, Lynn. I care about the community, too, and I'm going to catch the killer . . . or killers. I've done it for a long time, so I hope you'll trust that I know what I'm doing."

"You know that I also file stories in Boston papers, too. Mr. Bartlett is a prominent business man. His murder is news, Jack."

"I understand. I'm sorry I don't have more to give you."

She nodded and put the pen and pad into her purse. "I'll be in touch, Jack."

I watched as she turned and walked out, looking more like a local citizen than a reporter hot on a story. I hoped it would stay that way.

Chapter Eighteen

I was still in my office after lunch and was getting anxious. I hate being behind a desk all day, but I had to make some calls. One call was to the State Police in Framingham, where I relied on help from an old friend, Major Clint Hawkins, in charge of the Homicide Command. I told him about my cases and that I feared the Bartlett murder could be Mob related. He assured me he'd look into it and would alert the local barracks in South Yarmouth. I had a contact there, but I knew Clint from way back and felt that I'd get more cooperation from the local office if they heard from Major Hawkins first.

During my days with the METs, I often worked with the Federal Bureau of Investigation in the fight against organized crime in New England. Agent Nelson was my lead man. I had worked with him about a year ago to break up a neo-Nazi group in Marshfield and put Sal DiFino, aka Sammy White, right hand to Tommy Shea, behind bars. Shea headed up the Winter Hill boys from Somerville, a major bunch of thugs, killers, racketeers and drug dealers. My call to him was intended as a heads-up because of the possibility that Grant Bartlett might have had trouble with the Mob. He promised to keep his eyes and ears open and would get in touch with me if anything came up.

It was time to go to the Grant Bartlett's warehouse business. I took Officer Orlando with me. She was sure getting a load of experience with homicides.

We parked near the entrance and scanned in all directions as we made our way into the place. Once inside, we heard a clapping noise down one aisle of tall metal storage racks. Orlando and I glanced at each other and our hands went to the grips of our revolvers.

"Hello, anybody there?" I barked.

"Yeah. Over here. I'll be right with you."

Looking in the direction of the voice, I saw a rugged looking guy tossing some oak palettes into a pile. He moved up the aisle toward us and took off his leather gloves as he got closer, carrying them in his left hand.

"What can I do for you?" he asked.

He identified himself as Buck Nizzari, an employee of Grant Bartlett's.

We relaxed our hands. "I'm Detective Jack Contino and this is Officer Orlando. I'm afraid we have some bad news for you about Mr. Bartlett."

His dark eyes moved over Karen Orlando. "He's not in yet. I guess he's running late today."

"No, Mr. Nizzari, I'm afraid it's worse than that. Grant Bartlett was murdered last night."

His eyes shot back to me. "Holy shit. You kidding me or something? Mr. Bartlett? Murdered? What happened?"

"He was shot in the back and his body was dumped into the water off West Dennis Beach," said Officer Orlando.

Nizzari looked at Karen in an entirely different way this time. "Geeze, I don't know what to say. I can't believe it."

"Mr. Nizzari, did you work directly for Mr. Bartlett?" she asked. Orlando seemed comfortable asking the questions, so I let her run with it.

"Yeah, I'm the warehouse supervisor. I control any merchandise moving in or out. I got a couple of young guys who work here, too. You want to talk with them, too?"

"Maybe later," said Orlando. "Was Mr. Bartlett in the office yesterday?"

"Yeah, all day. He mostly stays in his office, doing paper work and making calls." Nizzari rubbed his hands on his pants.

"To your knowledge, Mr. Nizzari, was Bartlett having trouble with anyone?" Orlando had taken out her notepad and scribbled in it as he spoke.

"No, not that I know of. Of course, I don't know much about the business end of things, beyond handling the stuff coming in and out."

"Did he have any visitors recently?"

"Sure, sometimes some business looking types show up, you know the kind. They wear suits and ties and sun glasses. They even keep the sun glasses on inside. I don't get it."

"Were any of those types here yesterday?"

"No, not yesterday."

"Was there anybody else?"

"No, nobody else. Oh wait, there was a weird kind of guy standing outside Mr. Bartlett's office for a while. I came up to him and asked if I could help him and he said no, that he had a message for Mr. Bartlett. But he said Mr. Bartlett looked too busy, so he left, real quick, like I spooked him or something."

"What did this weird guy look like, Mr. Nizzari?"

His eyes scanned Orlando again, like he was scoring her for her looks. Her uniform pants were tight fitting and her shirt couldn't hide her breasts. I doubt that Buck Nizzari saw many good looking young women in the warehouse.

"Call me Buck."

"Okay, Buck, what did he look like?"

Nizzari's mouth made a slight grin at hearing Orlando say his first name. "He was maybe near six feet, a little chubby, I'd say."

"What about his facial features, Buck, his eyes, his hair?"

"I didn't really notice. I mean, he turned away real quick. I guess he was kind of plain looking."

"You mean you couldn't even tell what color his hair was?"

"No. Hell, he had on a hood, you know, on his sweatshirt, and he had it pulled tight over his head. I couldn't even see his hair, never mind tell what color it was."

Orlando and I stared at each other. "Buck," said Orlando, "what color was the sweatshirt and what about his pants?"

"It was dark, maybe dark blue, not black. His pants were blue jeans, just regular old blue jeans."

I swallowed hard as I pulled a folded copy of the sketch out of my coat pocket and opened it. I dangled it in front of Nizzari. "Did the guy look anything like this?"

Buck's eyes opened wider, one brow moving into a high arch above his eye. "Yeah, yeah, that could be him. It definitely could be him."

Orlando spoke quickly. "Buck, did anybody else see him?"

"No, the other guys were out back and the secretary was on break. I was the only one around, so I kept an eye out for the front door. I just got back from the men's room when I saw him."

"That's good, Buck. Thanks." Orlando eased a card out of her breast pocket and handed it to Nizzari. "Buck, I need you to call our office if that guy ever comes back."

"Sure, no problem, Officer Orlando. So, that's your office phone on the card?"

"Yes, Buck. Call that number anytime. You can talk to anybody. They'll get the message to us."

I also gave a card to Buck, shook his hand and thanked him. Orlando offered her hand. He clasped it gently with both of his, not shaking it. In a few seconds, we were in the car heading back to HQ.

"I don't believe this shit. Pardon me, Officer. This is too much. I know a lot of guys wear clothes like that, but it's just too much to be a coincidence."

"This guy's really getting around. What could possibly tie these murders together, Jack?"

"I don't know, Officer, but we're going to find out."

We rode in silence for a minute, letting the air clear a bit.

"By the way, I think you made quite an impression on Buck Nizzari," I said. "Maybe a friend for life."

Karen shot a look at me, the kind of look that says to a man, "Shut up."

Chapter Nineteen

Leo got back to me later in the day saying he had some interesting information about Back Bay Resources.

"It's a legit corporation, technically speaking, but it looks like a shady deal to me. It was incorporated the same year the Cape Cod Arena was built and it financed the construction. But guess who is a principal in the company. Good old Joe Vito, nightclub owner, head buster, boss to the late Ben Secani and well-established character in the Boston underworld. If Back Bay Resources is a legit enterprise, then I'm the Easter Bunny."

"So I guess we know where Back Bay gets its resources. Drugs, gambling, extortion, prostitution is their way of lining their bank account," I said.

"Too bad we can't prove it, Jack."

"Maybe someday we will, or somebody will. Right now, it's not my major concern."

"What gives, Jack? I thought you figured this to be a Mob hit and we definitely have a Mob connection now."

"Maybe we'll let Agent Nelson do the digging, Leo. I'm afraid I've got another avenue I have to travel down."

"I'm listening."

"Officer Orlando and I went to Bartlett's warehouse this morning. The warehouse manager told us there was a weird guy hanging around Bartlett's office the day before he was killed. He was big, a little chubby and wore jeans and a dark blue hooded sweatshirt pulled tight over his head."

"Geeze, Jack. That guy seems to be showing up in all your recent murder cases. Sounds like you've got a creep-of-the week type on Cape Cod. How do you figure this guy?"

Leo always found simple but effective ways of describing bad guys.

"So far, I don't figure him at all. Three murders with very little in common, except this guy in the hoodie sweatshirt and jeans is seen coming and going. We've got a clean-cut local merchant who gets shot, a female college teacher who gets bludgeoned and cut up and now a prominent businessman with apparent Mob ties gets shot and dumped in a river. Nothing adds up."

"Maybe you've just got a psycho on your hands."

"Maybe, but serial killers usually show a pattern. They all go after the same type of victim or they leave a trademark of some kind."

"In two of these killings, he used a gun."

"Yeah, Leo, we'll have a ballistics report pretty soon. But a match there can only confirm that those two may have been the work of the same guy. We already figure that to be the case."

"So you don't want to shake Joe Vito's tree?"

"No. Like I said, let the FBI do that if they want. I think I'd just be wasting my time and I can't afford that."

"You think these could all be contract hits, not a psycho?"

"It's possible, but there's got to be a strong connection with all the victims and I can't see one yet. Why kill the college teacher? I need to keep digging. The bodies are piling up so fast I can't stay on one case before I've got another one. And the local press is getting anxious."

"You want me to come down there to help out?"

"Thanks, Leo, but no. Stay home in Beantown for now. I've got State Police help if I need it."

"Okay, but just holler if things get worse."

"You got it, old pal."

If things got much worse, I might need ten guys like Leo.

Chapter Twenty

Come out, come out wherever you are. Come on, lady, get your ass out here. I can't sit in this lot forever.

Natalie was finishing her day at the doctor's office and realized she needed some odds and ends from the supermarket. She took a few minutes to write them down: artificial sweetener, milk, bread, cold cuts, toilet paper, a dessert for tonight.

Dr. David King emerged from his office, wearing a long white smock over an open-collar blue shirt and dark slacks. Natalie stopped writing when she noticed her boss watching her.

"I'm a list writer, Doctor. I've got to jot things down before shopping. It gives me a satisfied feeling, knowing I can check things off the list. I know I got everything."

"Understood," he said. "I do the same."

"Good night, Doctor," she called out as she tossed on her overcoat and grabbed her purse.

"Good night, Natalie. Tell Jack I should have his lab work in a couple of days. Don't let him forget to schedule the colonoscopy."

The word hit Natalie. "What? Jack needs a colonoscopy? He didn't tell me that."

"I told him when he had his physical that he needs one and to schedule it on your day off so you can drive him. He didn't tell you, huh?"

"No he didn't. I realize that he's very busy right now. He's got three homicides to investigate and he's quite worried about them."

"Three? I thought he said two."

"Oh, I'm afraid there was another one, Doctor."

"Wow, that's not good news. All of them in Dennis, I presume, since they're Jack's cases."

"That's right. It's very unusual for such a small town. But Jack's got a lot of experience with such things and that's good for Dennis. But it's also why we moved here, so he could have a slower pace than in Boston."

"So much for that, Natalie. Well, nonetheless, he needs to schedule that procedure soon."

"Oh, don't worry, Doctor, I'll get on him about it tonight, you can be sure of that."

"Good. And you can schedule one for yourself, too."

The rhythm of the conversation was broken by a short silence.

"Me?"

"Yes, Natalie, you both should have them. You shouldn't neglect your own health." Dr. King fought off the urge to smile.

"I guess . . . well, yeah, sure, of course. Got to go now. Bye."

Natalie quickened her pace out of the building and into the parking lot. She reached her mid-size green and white Plymouth, found her keys in her purse and opened the driver's door. After throwing her purse onto the passenger seat, she climbed in and started the engine.

The Plymouth didn't have far to go to reach the Stop and Shop. It was a sharp left turn at the intersection just outside the medical building and an immediate right turn into a larger lot where the super market and several specialty shops were located. She didn't notice the gray Chevy Nova that followed her from one parking lot into the other.

***

This is just so fucking cool. That dumb bitch doesn't even know I'm here. I love doing this stuff. I can just pick them and take them out. They're all mine, anyone, anytime, anyplace. Of course, this bitch is special. The guy doesn't even know that I can snuff out his old lady today. Fun, fun, fun.

***

Natalie grabbed a push cart from the collection at the entrance and moved into the store, heading for the far aisle to her right. She liked scanning the whole store even if she only had to buy a few things. Jack wouldn't be home for a while, so there was no hurry.

In a couple of minutes, her cart held several of the items on her list and a few extras. Passing by the meat section, she browsed the selections and a sign caught her eye. BUY ONE, GET ONE FREE, it said. Into the cart went two roaster chickens. The second fridge in the garage provided plenty of freezer space for such good deals. Jack loved to grill chicken with a half can of beer stuck into the cavity. He called it beer-can chicken, having learned that trick from Leo.

She's not bad looking for an old broad. Got to be in her fifties, at least. I wouldn't mind a little meat-grinding with her. Picking out a couple of birds, are you girl? Here, chickie, chickie.

After Natalie picked some pumpernickel bread, she had found everything on her list. She wanted a look at the produce section before leaving, however, so she swung her cart away from the checkout lines. As she turned, she didn't notice the nose of the other cart emerging from the next aisle and the light collision was unavoidable.

"Oh, I'm sorry," said the young woman in a police uniform, as the carts jarred together, nose to nose. The young officer recognized her victim. "Mrs. Contino, nice to see you. Are you okay?"

"Yes, yes. I'm fine. You're Karen Orlando, aren't you? I remember meeting you at the police station. What would Jack think if he knew we were having cart crashes at the supermarket?"

"Maybe that's why he keeps me off traffic duty, as much as possible."

"Speaking of Jack, I assume he is still in his office."

"Oh, yes. He's really working hard on these recent cases." Karen looked around and lowered her voice. "You know about them, right?"

"Yeah, and I can't believe there was another one this morning. I'm starting to wonder about Cape Cod. Maybe we should have moved to a quiet little town on the Maine coast. I'll bet they don't have many homicides up there."

Calculation   Steven P. Marini

🔫 🔫 🔫

Holy shit. It's the girly cop, right here with the guy's old lady. Shit, that screws things up a bit. Now, she's more my speed. I've never seen a cop fill out pants like that before. Don't look this way, honey. Don't make this complicated. Think I'll have to shop another aisle, for now. Damn, she sure can fuck up a wet dream. Maybe you'd be more fun, Officer Tight Pants. I know you would. Guess I'll wait in my car and watch for you to leave. Gotta see what you drive and follow you home. I got to learn where you live if I'm going to pay you a visit later on. Yeah, that'll be a fun visit.

Chapter Twenty-One

It was a little after six o'clock when I finally pulled into my driveway. It's always a great feeling of relief when I see the house and yard. Knowing it's your place, even if it's not the one you lived in for thirty some years, makes it a special place. There weren't any babies running around inside or making so much noise I could hear them from the driveway, but this house is now our home. The stress from a day's work eased out of my veins when I got here. It was a constant in the otherwise up-and-down existence of being a cop.

I barely got two feet inside when her voice struck me.

"Well, Detective Contino, have you forgotten something recently?"

"What, I don't think so. What do you mean?"

"Didn't Dr. King tell you to schedule a colonoscopy?"

"Oh, that."

"Yes, oh that. Jack, this is important business. You know, sometimes you're like a little boy. I have to pull teeth to get you to have a physical and then you're told to have a procedure and you try to push it off. I'm getting tired of having to pull you by the hand all the time. It's not just your life we're talking about, it's mine too, and the kids'. You're my husband and you're their father. We want and need you to be around for a while. Damn it, Jack, get with it. You're a grown man. I shouldn't have to do this all the time."

Her voice was near cracking. That got my attention.

"Whoa, Nat, calm down. I'll schedule the thing. Just give me some time. Look what's going on around here."

"I know, I know, but, damn it, Jack."

Her tone gave me a chill. "Hey, did the doc tell you something about my blood work that I need to know?"

"No, no, there's nothing unusual. But at your age, you have to watch out for colon cancer. After all you've been through, that we've been through, I don't want you getting a disease that could be prevented or detected early by a simple procedure."

I moved close to Natalie, looked down at her tiny figure standing in front of me, and took her in my arms. I wrapped one arm around her legs just below her butt and another around her upper back and lifted her, hugging her like a baby.

"Don't worry. I'll schedule the thing tomorrow, provided I don't get another surprise from our hooded friend."

Nat went limp in my arms, her hands clasped around my neck. "Jack, I can't stand the thought of losing you."

"You're not losing me. Hey, I'm healthy as a horse. But I'll get that thing, I promise. Say, did the doc mention anything else?"

"What?"

"He told me that you need one, too, and should schedule one sometime after mine."

"Jack, put me down."

I eased her down on her feet and she squirmed out of my arms. I stood there with my arms out to my sides, as if I was surrendering. "Well, that's what he said."

"Yes, he told me. Okay, so we both need one. Fine."

Sometimes it doesn't pay for a man to make fine points in a discussion with his wife. This conversation had to change. Move on, Jack.

Chapter Twenty-Two

A few more days passed by. I scheduled my colonoscopy with the gastroenterologist that Dr. King suggested, and I was pleased to hear that he couldn't fit me in for four weeks. I welcomed the breathing room.

There were two services held for Blake Hairston, one at her church and one at the college. I went to both. At the college service, I spoke to Dr. Hunter and Bob Anthony briefly. There had been a couple of reports by students about some guys in dark hooded sweatshirts, but they were bogus. It seems a couple of kids wanted to have some fun by turning in their buddy as a practical joke. Some girls were seeing guys in hoodies everywhere they looked, but none of them looked like they could shave, much less commit grizzly murders.

Jim Pearson looked in on Anne Schroeder and her daughter. There was nothing unusual going on there and she had reopened the liquor store. They appeared to have their lives under control, considering the circumstances.

It was about time to follow up with Buck Nizzari at the warehouse, but I didn't dare send Karen Orlando. I was afraid she might get an unwanted marriage proposal from her new admirer. I'd check in on him alone next time.

Jim Pearson went over his file of old cases from around Massachusetts. Jim kept a file of newspaper clippings and his own notes about homicides from anywhere in the state. He took them from all of the Boston newspapers and Providence, R.I., as well. Sometimes he managed to dig out helpful information, like similarities in M.O. But so far he couldn't find anything that looked like a link to the recent murders.

When you have fresh murders on your hands and then there's a lull, you get a cold feeling. If you are dealing with a serial killer, you fear that another murder will take place any day. It's like when your child gets very sick and you fear it will never stop and there isn't much you can do. I hated that feeling.

It was around two o'clock in the afternoon when I got a call from Leo.

"Hey Jack, I got some news for you. You remember Billy D'Agostino, the good rat from Somerville?"

I sure did. Billy was a successful extortionist and part of his success was getting protection from prosecution as long as he fed us good information about some of the Boston Mob scene.

"As a matter of fact, last year he bought a house on Bass River in your jurisdiction. I guess he felt better being near you, pal. Didn't he ever stop by to say hello?"

"Nope, he never did. Just as well, I wouldn't want to compromise your ongoing relationship with him."

"No need to worry about that, Jack, old boy. D'Agostino won't be making any more snitch reports for me or anybody else. He bought it big time this morning."

"No kidding. What happened?"

"He took a couple of rounds in the back of the head. They found him on the banks of the Charles near the sailboat docks before sun up. Maybe somebody blew his cover. Snitches don't have long life expectancies if they stick around too long. I guess he was past his expiration date."

Too bad for Billy. I always thought he was strictly small-time. But he had charm and he won over a lot of girls in the Combat Zone, who he joyfully shared with other mobsters as a way of winning their favor and the entrance fee into many a poker game. The girls took care of the players for free, and Billy didn't have to come up with the cash to get past the door. Sometimes he didn't even have enough dough to bet with, so he'd use a girl whose value was acknowledged by her special talents. He'd tell the girl to chat with her partner and report back to him, at which time Billy would slip her a few bucks. That's how he got information to relay on to the METs, namely me or Leo.

"Maybe one of his stable girls spoke out of turn and let the cat out of the bag about Billy, or he pissed one of them off and she did it intentionally," I said.

"I don't know, Jack, it's hard to say. We'll have to chat with some of those not so young ladies."

"So, he had a place here in Dennis. I never would have guessed."

"I'm telling you, Jack, he probably wanted to keep a connection with you. I bet he was going to show up at your door one of these days."

"Thank goodness he didn't. The last thing I need is to have guys like him following me to the Cape. Nat would have a fit. What a damned coincidence."

"That reminds me, Jack, what was it you often said about coincidences?"

"That they're often the result of planned occurrences. So you think that Billy had a plan, other than to be my neighbor?"

"I don't know, Jack. I just thought of that, is all."

"He didn't have any family, so I guess the funeral will be quiet. Let me know where and when and I'll see if I can make it."

"Okay, will do. Probably be just you and me."

"And maybe the shooter. Just kidding, Leo, just kidding. Thanks for calling. I appreciate the news."

"No problem, Jack. By the way, I still hope to make a weekend visit with you and Nat before the snow flies. That's assuming you're not tied up with those cases of yours."

"You're welcome here anytime, buddy, cases or no cases. You can always do a ride along with me."

"Wow, you really know how to sweeten the pot. How can I resist."

"Be cool, Leo. Talk to you later."

Geeze, a snitch followed me to Dennis. I hope nobody else is following me around.

Chapter Twenty-Three

He picked up the old newspaper and brushed his hand over the folded front page as if caressing an old flame. The headline was bold and straight forward and he loved to read it over and over again: *Prominent Cape Businessman Slain*

It took them a while to finally pay some attention. This is much better. I have to admit that I'm rather proud of this one, considering that the Neanderthal in the warehouse spooked me a bit. I didn't let that stop me, though, did I? Bounced right back, I did. Ah, nothing like grace in the face of adversity. Maybe I should frame this one. No, I'll cut out the story eventually for my scrapbook, but I kind of like keeping it whole for now. It helps keep the story alive. Hah, hah. Ain't that a kick.

He walked into the small kitchen in the Hyannis apartment, rinsed out a large mug in the sink and poured a cup of strong coffee from the small coffee maker on the counter.

Where's the sugar? Ah, there you are. Sweets for the sweet. That's me, sweet as can be. Now the cow.

He opened the fridge and grabbed the plastic milk bottle by the handle, adding some of its contents into his drink. His middle finger served as a suitable stirrer, which he sucked clean. It seemed to amuse him. He stretched his heavy frame on the sleep sofa, took two sips of his coffee and put the mug down on an end table badly in need of refinishing.

Well now. I certainly do have a decision to make. Mrs. Cop would have been a nifty little prize. But now we have Officer Tight Pants in the picture and I must admit she's got me in a pickle. She's just too good to pass up. And besides, how many police departments have got an Officer Tight Pants, really? And here we are with our very own in good old Dennis, working with the big guy. My, my, my. Oh, thank you little lady cop. You've made me so happy. I'll have to think of something extra special for you. Maybe something slow and nice, so you'll know what's happening, so you can appreciate the skill and creativity that goes into my work. And I'll get to enjoy Officer Tight Pants without her pants. Oh, yes indeed. This is feeling so good already.

His right hand went to his crotch, moving over his jeans.

Soon this will be your hand, my girl. Should I keep your hand attached for the job? Hah, hah, hah.

He worked his husky frame off the sofa after having a good laugh and walked over to his dresser, opened the bottom drawer and pulled out another old copy of the local newspaper, his eyes drawn to the story on the bottom of the front page, "Local Man Testifies in Marshfield Murder."

Must not get ahead of myself, now. Tight Pants will be there when you are ready for her. Just slide her into the queue. Hah, hah, I bet she slides real nice and easy, too. But first things first. This bartender fellow has to play his part, too. Pay him a visit and work on him a bit. But how much work? Should he die? To die, to sleep. To sleep perchance to dream. Or maybe just cut him up a bit. Whatever. It will certainly get the big cop's attention. He really doesn't have a clue yet, does he? Let's see, Mr. Bartender is a talker, says so right here. You can't testify in court without talking. I think he's talked enough. Maybe he needs to go quiet, forever.

Chapter Twenty-Four

He usually avoids going off Cape during the summer. On a Sunday afternoon it is automotive torture. But a fall afternoon makes for an almost relaxing drive over the Sagamore Bridge, and up Rte. 3. Even the Southeast Expressway is tame, not what it will be like on Monday morning rush hour.

Once in a while, he had the urge to visit Beantown. It was more than just an urge. It was a compulsion. The Combat Zone, that sleezy section of adult entertainment centered along Washington Street, with multiple bars and strip clubs, held a special allure for him. The big boys were there.

Club 77 was his target. He learned a lot about who ran the place and who hung out there. Joe Vito, the owner, was a major player in the Boston Mob. His chief bartender, Big Ted, all six-foot ten inches of him, looked like an escapee from the National Basketball Association. But his main reason for going there was Tommy Shea, top dog in the Winter Hill Gang from Somerville.

His aging Nova fit in well with many of the banged-up, paint-fading cars parked along Washington Street. He squeezed his Chevy into a curbside spot two blocks away and opened the driver-side door, then pulled himself out of it and sauntered onto the sidewalk. The air was cool, so he pulled up the hood of his tattered, dark sweatshirt, jammed his hands into the pockets and made his way to Club 77.

He smiled at the sound of the recorded music playing, which meant a topless dancer was moving her goodies to the beat on an elevated dance platform. He kept his eyes down when he entered the dim establishment, allowing them to adjust to the darkness. He didn't want to look like those college kids and military guys, first time visitors to the place, whose eyes went immediately to the nearly naked dancer on the platform. He was no rookie.

After taking two steps inside, another feeling raced through his veins. There was a large round table off to his right, with men and women talking loudly. He could hear the sound of voices, one in particular. Tommy Shea was holding court, as he often did, at the table by the door. *My main man.*

He waited until he planted himself on a barstool before he glanced at the dancer, bumping, grinding and go-going on the platform. *Mighty nice body for an older chick. Someday, lady, someday.*

"You drinking today or just here for the floor show?" Big Ted's deep voice cut through the music with authority.

He spun his stool back toward the bar, eyeing the huge man in front of him. "I'll have a beer. You got Miller on tap?"

Big Ted didn't answer. He just grabbed a pilsner glass and slid it under the tap. He drew the drink perfectly, leaving an inch of head at the top. "You running a tab?"

"Ah, yeah, sure. When did Ginny become a blonde?"

"When the boss told her to." Ted looked at the guy for a second, trying to place the face. In a slow movement, he leaned on the bar with both elbows, his face a foot away from the guy drinking his beer. "Sounds like you know Ginny."

"I've been here before, watched her dance. She's a great dancer. I love her moves."

"Ginny has many talents, but you probably already know that."

"No doubt about it. She sure has the right equipment."

"Her dance set will be over in a couple of minutes. For a guy with some cash in his pockets, she could be persuaded to demonstrate her talents in a little room out back. It's real private and comfortable. You interested?"

I'm starting to get interested, big fella. I hadn't counted on this.

"What's the price of special talent today?"

"You put fifty under your glass and I'll give her the word."

There was a pause and Ted figured the customer wasn't carrying a bundle. "Okay, twenty-five and she shows you how well she plays a wind instrument." Ted's eyes went to the guy's right hand as it slid away from the glass and went into his pants pocket. He drew out his cash and the money went under the glass as instructed.

"I . . . got to use the men's room."

Ted motioned and the guy slid off the stool and disappeared for a few minutes. When he returned, the money was gone and the music stopped. He exchanged looks with Ted and climbed back onto his perch, his elbows on the bar. Suddenly he heard a female voice and her arm reached over his shoulder. "Thanks, Teddy Boy." Ted slipped some cash into her hand while she pressed her breasts against the customer, her left hand on his shoulder. She whispered something into his right ear and sashayed away, deeper into the darkness.

Her customer focused on Ginny's forty-plus-year old ass. She kept in great shape, her legs and buttocks still firm and trim. He dropped off the bar stool, followed her slowly and thought about what was to come.

He saw her go inside the back room, flip on the lights and adjust them low with a dimmer switch. His pace quickened as he followed her. Ginny held the door for him and swung her free arm in a gesture to enter. The room was not what he expected. There was a round table in the middle, suitable for business meetings or poker games. A full size refrigerator was in one corner next to a cherry wood liquor cabinet. At the far end was a large sofa.

"You know, you are way overdressed, young man." She stood in front of him, pressing her breasts against him and loosened the hood of his sweatshirt, pushing it down to his neck.

"So are you, sweet cheeks," he said.

"Hah. You're the first guy who's ever accused me of that. Pasties and a G-string usually don't qualify for formal wear. I guess I can lose some of it." She flipped off the pasties and dropped them on the table.

He enjoyed her every move. She eased herself down to her knees to help him out of his sneakers and socks. At the same time, he ripped off his sweatshirt and the red T under it, revealing his pudgy, pale body. As her hands caressed his thighs, he looked at her, anticipating their destination. He wanted to grab her, but as her hands moved over his crotch, he went weak from pleasure. Her fingers worked at his belt, opening it and unsnapping his jeans. She pushed them down over his legs. He placed a hand on her shoulder for balance as he stepped out of them. She did the same with his shorts. He couldn't remember the last time he was naked with a woman.

"Don't you dare move, big boy. Just stand there. Ginny's going to take good care of you. Just close your eyes and think good thoughts." He obeyed her commands and stood still, arms by his sides. He felt her hands move up his body, onto his chest and over a shoulder as she circled him. Her hands pressed his back and she shifted from palms to fingertips when she reached his buttocks. She scratched at them lightly and let a finger tease between his cheeks. When she circled back in front, she dropped to her knees once more and he felt her hands rise up along his bare thighs. He let out a whimper as he felt her hand clutch him. His erection pulsated as she caressed it with a finger and eased it into her mouth. In less than a minute, Ginny earned her money.

He stood there naked and drained. His pleasure was complete, but he kept his eyes closed, extending the experience as long as he could.

"Take your time getting dressed, big boy," said Ginny, her voice growing faint as she scooped up her pasties and scampered from the room.

When he opened his eyes, he was alone. He gathered up his clothes and put them on, drawing his shorts up first, then he sat in a chair at the table to pull on his socks, pants and shoes. He slid into the T-shirt and finally zipped into his dark, hooded sweatshirt, tightening the hood on his head, but not tying the drawstring under his neck.

With the physical excitement over, he was overtaken by emptiness. Alone in the back room, he could hear the dance music playing again. Ginny had moved on to her next dance.

Think you're pretty good, don't you, bitch? All in a day's work for you, huh. Maybe someday you'll get to sample my work. Now, that would be cool, really cool. Only I won't be paying next time. You will. There are all kinds of things I could do with you, sweet stuff. You won't go rushing out on me then, wait and see. All right, it's you, Ginny, not some stuck up college bitch. I'll give you that. But you need to show me a little respect, too, you know. Maybe I'll give you the chance. Maybe.

As he walked back to the bar, he saw Big Ted give him a glance. "Not bad, eh, pal? Like I said before, Ginny has many talents. I freshened up your beer. This one's on the house."

He took his place on the bar stool and sipped the fresh draught. The cool sensation of the swallow relieved the dryness in his throat. He sipped some more.

"Man, you look intense, pal," said Ted. "Most guys come back here with their eyes crossed after a time with Ginny. Relax and enjoy the beer."

He raised his head slowly. "Yeah, yeah, I am. Ginny was great, really great."

"Yo, Ted," came a voice from the table near the door. "I'm getting dry over here. Send another round."

He knew immediately that the voice belonged to Tommy Shea. *Nobody else would bark an order like that to Big Ted. Tommy Shea, leader of the Winter Hill boys and the smartest, toughest guy in town. Yes, sir, now there's a man for you.*

"Got you," said Ted. "Coming right up."

"Put that round on my tab and I'll square up now. I gotta get going."

"Sure, why not," said Ted. He poured the drinks and gave them to a waitress to deliver to Shea's table, then took the money from the customer in the jeans and hoodie. "Well, I'll be. Looks like you were carrying more dough than I thought. You know, you could have had more time with Ginny if you . . . ah, what the hell. Your choice."

He spun off the bar stool and headed for the door, watching as the waitress put the drinks on Shea's table and told him who paid for them. He smiled tightly at Shea, who sat motionless, eyeing the man as he walked out.

"Hey Tommy, you know that guy?" asked one of the girls at the table.

Shea shot back his answer. "Who I know or don't know is none of your fucking business. Don't forget that."

Tommy motioned with his finger to the man seated across the table. The two got up and walked to the door and out onto the sidewalk. They looked both ways in a hurry and finally Tommy spotted the dark hooded sweatshirt on the guy who just bought him a drink. He tapped his friend on the shoulder and gave him a command. The friend, Bobby Sullivan, raced down the street to get within a close distance before the man got away. Bobby stopped when he saw the man step into the street between two cars and look back. Then the guy was inside a gray Nova and pulling away. Bobby could see the license plate clearly and memorized the number until he could pull a pen and small pad out of his pocket.

Sullivan wrote down the plate number and returned to Club 77. He resumed his seat at the table and slipped the paper to Tommy Shea. Tommy read it and crunched the paper as he put it in his pocket.

"Good work, Bobby. I'll take care of it from here."

"What do you think, Tommy? Is this somebody trying to set you up for something, or maybe trying to get on your good side for a deal?"

Shea didn't answer his friend's questions. He got up from the table and strutted up to a place at the bar, away from customers. Big Ted put down the glass he was wiping and went over to Shea. Ted relayed the short story of the man's visit to the Club and his time with Ginny.

"Did he say why he wanted to buy me a drink?"

"No, I figured maybe he knows you. He knew who Ginny was, so I guess he's been here before. I figured you wouldn't mind a freebie."

"You didn't get his name?"

"Nope. I was just thinking about getting him laid. The way he was looking at Ginny, I figured he was dying for it and I'd get my share. He was only up for a blow job, though, so it wasn't worth the effort. Hey, you want me to check with Mr. Vito?"

"When Ginny's done dancing, send her over. Yeah, check with Joe. I want to make sure there's nothing going on here, that's all."

"Got it."

A few minutes later, Ginny was sitting at a table near the back. It was a private enough area for Shea. Ginny pulled a wrap around her shoulders, the colors matching her pasties and G-string.

"Hey, he's just a John off the street, for all I know, and a cheap one at that. All he'd pay for was a BJ. I don't think he gets a lot of action, you know. He got it up in a heartbeat. I was afraid he was going to pop when I grabbed his nuts. Flabby bastard, but he had a cute dick."

"Ted says he knew you. He didn't say anything?"

"Lots of customers know my name. That doesn't mean they know me. Say anything? He could barely stand up. Talk about making a quick buck."

"Okay, Ginny." Shea motioned with his head for her to move on. This was probably nothing for Shea. But a guy can't be too sure.

Chapter Twenty-Five

I sure got Tommy's attention today. Not everybody's got the balls to buy him a drink. But I'm a guy he can count on. That's for sure. One of these days, Tommy boy, we're going to have a sit down. Yes sir, you and me are going to talk.

It was getting dark by the time he reached the Sagamore Bridge. He turned down the volume on his car radio so he could hear his own thoughts.

I couldn't believe the look on their faces when I waved at Tommy. They almost shit. Tommy was cool, though. Of course he was. Shit, he's the coolest guy in Beantown, not to mention Somerville and its famous Winter Hill section. Even those Boston Mafia guys don't screw with Tommy. They know what they'd get if they did. He's my man and soon I'm going to be HIS man. I'm proving it a little more with all my ... projects, shall we say. Man, this is GREAT.

His foot pressed down a little harder on the gas pedal as his Nova crossed over the bridge and was *officially* on the Cape again. The engine sputtered, as it labored to pull the little Nova up the next hill. He had more thinking to do.

I'm on a roll, man. I'm on a roll. Maybe this is a good time to visit that big mouth at the Sand Dune. Sunday night. Shouldn't be too busy. Yeah, why not? I'm psyched for it. Even got my tool kit handy in the trunk. Sorry, Hyannis exit, I got to keep on moving. Dennis, here I come. Exit nine it is. Boy, is that rat going to get a surprise.

🔫🔫🔫

The Sand Dune stayed opened until the end of October. In November, the owner closed for the season and headed north to Vermont ski country and his other establishment, the Ski Boot at Killington. George Rogers used to make the seasonal change of locations with him, but that was a long time ago. After getting married and having kids, he had to stay on the Cape and make a good enough living for his family. Bartending became his part-time occupation. Sometimes he missed the old days when youth made him carefree and following the beach crowd to ski country was an annual ritual.

The Cape Cod Mall offered several places to carve out a retail career and allowed for a firm schedule, the thing that gave him a chance to keep connected to the Sand Dune as a part-timer. It was a good life, all in all. The only bad time was getting stuck in that trap involving Sidney Fish, a drunken braggart who came in one night and gave George an earful about cutting up a Marshfield cop, a black female. He did the right thing, though, because he had to. It was right. He went to the cops and told the big detective about it. When Fish went on trial, George had to testify. It made his wife proud, though, when she saw his name in the papers. He was glad that was over.

🔫 🔫 🔫

The Chevy Nova slowed to a crawl as he pulled it into the Sand Dune parking lot, its tires crunching across the clamshell surface. There were only five cars in the small lot, one of them parked near the back, a few feet away from a large trash dumpster that sat about twenty feet from the back door. He pulled past the car near the dumpster and backed in beside it, so that his Nova was facing the parking lot exit, poised for a quick getaway. He turned off the engine and sat behind the wheel for a while.

After running several scenarios for murder through his head, he pulled his keys from the ignition and vacated the Nova, heading for the front entrance to the quiet drinking establishment. He made the usual adjustment to his attire, pushing the hood up on his head, pulling the drawstrings tight but not tying them under his chin. *Show time.*

Once inside, he stood momentarily inside the entrance, surveying the room. There were two men at the bar, seated in the center area, chatting and glancing at a TV mounted above the shelves of liquor. A single female, forty-something, sat two bar stools to the left of them. Her tight-fitting black dress seemed too much for a Sunday night, but her exposed thighs pleased him. A foursome sat at a square table near the rear windows, two couples about his own age, he imagined. An older looking couple, streaks of gray in each one's hair, sat at another table, the man's hands reaching across the table and clasped over the woman's. A bored looking cocktail waitress was at the service end of the bar.

How sweet, the old shits, smiling like a couple of lovesick teenie boppers. I want to puke. Move up to the bar, maestro, you're in charge now. Miss Sweet Thighs at the bar is sending a clear message. Nice to look at, but I won't be bothering with the likes of her tonight. Old Ginny girl took care of that. She sure knows how to clean your tubes, that Ginny. The waitress could be fun.

The bar took an L-shaped turn at the far left end and he selected the first stool after the corner, giving him a clear view of all patrons. An occasional lean to his right brought Sweet Thigh's charms into focus. The gray streaks were almost past his corner eye view, but he didn't much care about them anyway.

George Rogers approached the new customer. He wore a white shirt with blue stripes and a bow tie, black slacks and black shoes, a bartender look from another era.

"What can I get you, sir?"

Sir. Damned right you better call me sir. Always respect those who control your destiny.

"Got Miller on tap?"

"You bet." George turned away to grab a tall glass, place it under the tap and draw the beer.

"It must be getting chilly outside," he said to the customer.

"What makes you say that?"

"Well, with the sweatshirt and hood up, you know. Looks like you came in from a brisk night."

"Naw, it's not so bad. I'm just in my comfortable stuff, that's all." He drew a slow sip from his glass, wiping his upper lip with his tongue after.

"I don't think I've seen you here before. Your first time in?"

"No, I've been here a few times, but not a lot. I took in the show once or twice."

"Rick's been doing this for a long time. He plays a mean boogie-woogie piano, doesn't he?"

He scanned the area behind the bar, too consumed with his task of assessing the layout to make a reply. "You must have been busy today, by the looks of all that cardboard on the floor back there."

An opened doorway led from the bar to a back room and he figured the rear door across from the dumpster was there.

"Oh, yeah, the bottled beer comes in cardboard cases, just like in the package stores. I guess I'd better put those out in the dumpster pretty soon before I forget. The trash guys will be here early tomorrow morning."

He nodded and a grin emerged on his face. *Opportunity knocks. Yes indeed, take that trash out right away. The dumpster calls.*

He grabbed his glass and took a gulp. "I got to get something in my car. Be right back. Don't drink my beer, now."

George forced a chuckle and nodded. He gave the bar a wipe with a hand towel and surveyed the other customers for possible refills. The two guys at the bar ordered another round, but Sweet Thighs declined, so he filled the order and went about the task of collecting the cardboard.

The night really is getting cold, he thought, opening the trunk of the Nova and flipping the lid on a small black tool box. He drew out a six inch, fixed blade hunting knife in its sheath and gazed at it like a loving parent dotes on a child. He fastened the sheath to his belt, right side, closed the trunk of his Nova and leaned on it with his elbows, turning his gaze toward the dumpster.

Don't make me wait on you, Mister Big Mouth Witness.

He ran his hand over the sheath, caressing it with fingertips a few times before switching to a palm rub, then back to fingertips. *Maybe I should be putting notches in my belt. This could be another notch, just like in the old west. I knock one off, I notch the belt. Why not? I'll do that later. No time now. Maybe I should get closer. Too much noise when I walk over this seashell stuff.*

He walked smoothly, taking long strides and looking around at every step. There was a tall lattice partition jutting out from the back of the building, providing a degree of cover and dressing up the rear of the property a little. He took a position behind the lattice on the parking lot side and listened for movement.

He stood perfectly still for several long minutes before starting to finger the knife and the sheath again. *Notches.*

Yeah, notches would be good. His thought was broken by the sound of the back door being opened. He was startled by a bunch of cardboard cases that came flying out. George Rogers emerged soon after, carrying a few more. He carried them to the dumpster and raised his arms up, dropping them in through the top opening.

Okay. Okay. Do it. He slid the knife out of the sheath and held it in a tight fist. George turned to fetch the remaining cases, unprepared for the assault. The patron-turned-attacker was on him and thrust his knife into his target's midsection. He watched as his victim clutched his belly, blood oozing out through his fingers, and fell to the ground, emitting a low groan. He bent over his bleeding victim and withdrew the blade.

"Yeah baby. I'm your man, TOMMY SHEA. I'm your man."

He realized that his uncontrolled outburst may have alerted the bar patrons, so he ran to the gray Nova, knife still in hand. He fumbled to open the driver-door, threw the knife on the passenger seat and jumped in. The old car started quickly and in a few seconds he was out of the parking lot and on his way.

Yeah, baby. Yeah, baby. I'm your man, Shea. I'm your man.

When he got to Lower County Road, he turned right when he meant to turn left, east not west. *Okay. Okay. Doesn't matter. Throw them off better this way. Just get to Rte. 28 and turn. Oh, baby. Wow.* His chest was pounding as he made his course correction and headed back to his Hyannis apartment. *What a day, Tommy Shea. Hey, you, too Ginny. Thanks for pumping me up.*

Chapter Twenty-Six

Natalie carried the dinner dishes to the counter next to the sink, placing them at my side as I ran the water for a warm rinse. My eyes followed her as she turned away to finish clearing the small table in the corner. They call it a breakfast nook, but it serves very well as a dinner table for the two of us. She wore tight jeans with hip pockets and had the cuffs rolled up to her ankles. I conjured up an image of Dale Evans in her western jeans, not nearly as snug as what Nat wore. My smile betrayed me.

"What are you so pleased about, Detective?" asked Nat when she returned to the kitchen.

"What? Do I look pleased? Well, of course I do. I'm home with you."

"You certainly have the right answer handy . . . most of the time. But I think there's something sinister behind that smile."

"I have to admit, the rolled cuffs on those great fitting jeans reminded me of Dale Evans. Don't ask me why. You've got a lot more going for you. It just brought a smile, that's all."

"I know you too well, Jack Contino." She stood a few feet away from me and turned her back, bending slightly at the waist. "If you were thinking western, by chance were you dreaming about some bareback riding? Don't answer that. Tell you what, cowboy. Finish rinsing those dishes and putting them into the washer, and meet me in the bunkhouse."

I grabbed a dish towel from the counter and snapped it hard against her tail. "Yee-hah."

Nat gave out a high pitched yip and skipped away like a kid with a hobby horse between the legs. I scrambled to finish loading the dishwasher, humming "Happy Trails to You" as I did.

When I entered the bedroom, Nat was standing beside the bed, her jeans and panties on the floor, her back to me.

Calculation

Steven P. Marini

She looked at me over her shoulder as she unbuttoned her blouse. She had plenty of time to have gotten completely undressed and into bed, so I figured she waited for me like this, adding some spice to the action.

I eased my way up to her from behind and helped her with the rest of the buttons. Leaving the blouse on, I slid my hands across her wonderfully flat stomach and inched them upward to her breasts. Her bra was gone. I hadn't even noticed it on the floor beside the other clothes. My hands cupped each breast gently, followed by a caress. My fingers slid over her hardened nipples while I nuzzled her neck. I took hold of the blouse at her shoulders, pulled it down over her arms, and dropped it beside the rest of her outfit.

Nat never moved from her place, signaling me that she wanted more of what I was giving. My palms slid down her back and up again before I moved to her side. My left hand continued caressing her back while my right hand found her front, one beautiful breast, then the other. She felt exquisite, as always.

She spoke as she turned toward me. "You come through these parts often, cowboy?"

My hand slid to her inner thighs and between. "Not often enough . . . through these parts, dear lady."

Her hands began working on my belt and I undid my shirt. In a moment, I was naked with my dream girl and we held hands as we made our way onto our bed.

When we had finished our lovemaking, we lay in each other's arms for several minutes. There was a time, after the shooting, when we had to avoid sex for too long. Eventually, as I healed, we got it back. Now, we appreciated these times more than ever.

"I love you, Jack Contino, as much as ever," she said, her head on my chest.

"That's what keeps me going, sweetie. You're my life."

I felt myself nodding off, so I fought the sleep away. *It's too early. I'll be up all night if I snooze now.* After a trip to the bathroom, I got dressed and saw Nat was asleep in the bed.

"Hey, sweetie, you sure you want to do that?"

She groaned and stretched her arms up over her head. "Of course I want to do that. But you're right. I'd better get up."

Calculation
Steven P. Marini

I wished every Sunday night could be this good, a peaceful day, a great dinner and a seduction from my wife. Time for a drink, I decided, and I'd relax for the night. I went into the kitchen, got a highball glass and grabbed a handful of ice from the freezer. As I dropped the cubes into the glass, I realized how much I enjoyed the sound of ice hitting the empty glass. I didn't enjoy the sound of the telephone.

I hated this one. I hated driving up to another homicide scene, yellow tape already in place. What I hated most of all was having to leave home on a Sunday night after a very special time with Nat. I hated the look on her face when I told her. We'd been through times like this before, but it was different then. It was when my career was in full throttle and I believed, no, we believed, I was making a difference, a needed contribution to society.

Karen Orlando and three other officers were on scene. She broke off her interview with a couple seated at a small table. They looked older than most patrons at the Sand Dune. Maybe they were a throwback to the sixties, when Rick, the owner, was in his heyday and they had been regulars here. She looked tired.

"I've got good news and bad news, Jack. What'll it be?"

"Give me the bad, so I'll have something to look forward to." What possible good news could there be?

"The bartender, George Rogers, you remember him, was attacked outside after waiting on a customer at the bar. The woman seated at the bar said she heard them talking about throwing out some trash and the customer said he had to go out to his car for something. George went out back just after the guy left. A few minutes later, the waitress heard a voice yelling something from out there. She found George on the ground and bleeding badly. You're not going to like the next part."

"Like I'm enjoying this up 'til now? Go on."

"The guy yelled something about Tommy Shea."

I stood frozen for a moment. "Are you sure about that?"

"Ask her yourself. That's what she said she heard."

I felt my fingers tighten into a fist. It was an involuntary action, a reflex whenever I heard that name.

"It gets worse, Jack." She went from looking tired to apologetic.

"You're kidding. How can it get worse than Tommy Shea?"

Orlando looked at the floor for a second. Lifting her head up, she scanned the room. I thought she was looking for an escape route. "The witnesses all said that this guy was tall, a heavy set type and was wearing jeans and a dark, hooded sweatshirt, with the hood pulled up on his head."

She looked at me like she had just made a confession. She said she had bad news. Boy, she wasn't kidding.

I lowered my voice and leaned down to her. "Our hoodie guy did this? Our guy? And he's connected to Tommy Shea?"

Karen nodded, her lips shut tight.

Throughout this killing spree with Mr. Hoodie, I thought I was looking for a psycho, the worst kind of criminal. They have no sane reason for killing. They have no loyalties to protect, no logical gain to pursue, nothing that could make their actions easily predictable.

But I was wrong. If this psycho was involved with Shea, anything was possible. Shea was organized crime, but he was a nut case from day one, as far as I was concerned. He was a hair trigger who went off at anything that rubbed him the wrong way. But Shea hired professional killers, guys whose moves were calculated to do a job. This didn't fit, not at all.

I pounded my right fist against my leg repeatedly. When I got control, I looked at Orlando. "Is it time for the good news yet?"

"Jack, the victim is still alive, just barely, but alive. You'll notice the M.E. is not here. They took him to the hospital. Looks like a deep stab wound. It's too early to tell if he's going to make it."

The feeling of relief rushed through me like a jet. George had been reluctant to testify a year ago against Sidney Fish, but he did it. That took courage. Now, some wild man attacks him for what, for fun? What could Tommy Shea have to do with it?

The cocktail waitress introduced herself as Gail Devereaux. She was sitting at a table against the side wall, shivering, her hands folded in her lap. Her fingers were in constant motion, rubbing against each other and tears filled her eyes.

She was wearing a short, dark skirt and a short-sleeved white blouse. Maybe that was a good choice of attire to start the evening, but now everything had gone cold for her.

"Miss, don't you have a jacket or a sweater to put on? You're freezing."

"There's . . . there's one hanging up in the back." She turned her head in the direction of the back exit, where George had piled up the trash.

"Okay, I'll get it. Be right back."

I fetched her red windbreaker. It wasn't much, but it would help. I wrapped it around her shoulders.

"The woman officer talked to you before but, if you could, I'd like you to repeat what you heard and saw for me. Can you do that?"

She nodded and sniffled at the same time. "I was standing at the service bar, keeping an eye on the customers to see if they needed a refill. George had been talking to this guy at the other end of the bar for a while. Then he came back here and went out into the area where you got my jacket. The other guy got up and left and said something to George about being right back. So, I can hear George gathering up some cardboard trash and he opened the back door. I heard some noise, but didn't think much of it, figuring it was just George throwing the trash into the dumpster. Then I heard this voice saying something, "I'm your man, Tommy Shea," or something like that."

"Miss, are you sure about that name?"

"Yes, definitely, it was Tommy Shea. I'm sure of that. He yelled it out pretty loud."

"What did you do when you heard all this?"

"I went out by the door to take a look. I saw George lying on the ground, bleeding. I screamed and ran to him. I heard a car pull out of the parking lot, but I didn't see it. I just wanted to help George, so I ran inside and called for an ambulance. We keep emergency numbers by the phone behind the bar. I grabbed a towel and brought it out with me and pressed it against his stomach, where he was bleeding. I learned that in a first aid film in school, how to put pressure on a wound to slow the bleeding. I know it didn't take long for the ambulance to arrive, but it seemed like forever.

George was still alive when they took him away. I hope he's going to live. Have you heard? Is he going to live?" She was shaking, like she was about to collapse.

I put an arm around her shoulders and held her until she calmed a bit. "No, I don't know yet. But you helped him a lot. You did the right thing with that towel. Is his home phone number on that list?"

"Yes. Do ... you ... want me to call his wife?"

"Oh, no, Miss. We'll do that. Don't worry."

Her pulse must have dropped a little because she seemed to be steadying after I spoke. I motioned for Karen Orlando to come over. "George Roger's home number is on an emergency list at the bar phone. Call his wife and tell her I'll meet her at the hospital. Stay with Miss Devereaux. When she's okay, give her a ride home. I want to talk to the woman at the bar and then I'm going to the hospital."

"Okay, Jack. Got it."

The woman witness was Barbara Carol. Besides making a weak joke about having two first names, she didn't have much to add from what she gave to Orlando. She was pretty tanked up and the night's events didn't seem to bother her much. She'd ride home courtesy of the Dennis Police. I had the officers get the names and contact information from all the other witnesses and I started for the hospital. I hoped George Rogers could help me one more time. I wish I could have helped him.

Chapter Twenty-Seven

When I got to the hospital in Hyannis, George Rogers was still in surgery so all I could do was wait. I decided to grab a coffee from the cafeteria, but all that was available was machine brew. What the heck, it's better than nothing, so I went for it.

By the time I got back to the waiting area, George's wife was at the admission counter. I gulped some coffee and damned near roasted my throat. I looked around for a place to put it down and didn't find one, so I held it and walked up to the frantic woman. She was pleading with the attendant for news about her husband.

Funny how you can recognize a face easily, especially after you had been used to seeing it often for a while, due to a case and court proceedings. Her first name was on the tip of my tongue and wouldn't move. I remembered the worried look on her face each day that George had to testify. Tonight her face was beyond worried.

When I reached the admission counter, I found a home for my coffee, which was starting to sting my hands. I placed it carefully, watching not to spill anything. When I looked back toward her, she caught sight of me and stepped in my direction.

"Oh, Jack, I'm so glad you're here." She stopped in front of me, looking into my eyes, clasping her hands in front of her as if in prayer. She put her head down and collapsed against me. I took hold of her, my arms around her narrow shoulders. We held the embrace for a moment. It doesn't take long for something peaceful to break into something else.

She broke the embrace and stepped back. Her right hand made a short backswing and reversed itself into a full throttle slap at my chest. "Oh, Jack, how could you let this happen? I knew he shouldn't have testified against that mobster. They were going to get him. I knew it. I just knew it."

I let the second slap happen before I clutched her hand gently and tried to wrap an arm around her shoulders again. She resisted, so I let go.

"Calm down, Jill. You've got to be calm." The tip of my tongue had freed itself. "Let's go sit."

There was an empty sofa a few feet away. I gestured in that direction and she complied. When we reached it and took seats, she snapped open her small purse and groped inside, finally extracting a clutch of tissues. She dabbed them against her sniffling nose.

"Jill, we don't know who did this. It happened at the Sand Dune while George was on duty."

"Yes, I'm aware of that. How did it happen?"

"Some guy was talking to him at the bar and said he had to get something from his car. So he went outside at the same time George took some trash out to the dumpster. We think the guy stabbed George and fled before anyone saw him."

"You mean this guy was waiting for George at the dumpster? That sure sounds calculated to me, Jack. My God, you're practically admitting this was a setup. Who would have a reason to do this except those mobsters?" She sniffled into her tissues, avoiding my eyes.

"Jill, the man George testified against is in prison. The one who hired that guy is dead. There's no way anyone else would be after George."

The sniffling stopped and Jill looked at me. She seemed to be reasoning it out in her head. "You really think so?"

"I do."

"I don't know, Jack. It all seems just too coincidental."

Coincidences are often the result of planned occurrences.

I wanted to tell her about Mr. Hoodie, but then she'd conclude there was a homicidal maniac running loose on the Cape. I didn't think that would make her feel better. *Oh, don't worry, Jill. Your husband wasn't attacked by vengeful mobsters. It was just a maniac with a knife. There's a lot of that going around.* I couldn't tell her the guy yelled something about Tommy Shea. That would cement her belief about the Mob.

I patted her near shoulder while she handled the tissue and looked away from me. She didn't know what to think and I didn't know what else I could tell her.

When a doctor in scrubs appeared and called her name, I got an idea how death row inmates must feel when the priest shows up. *This is it.*

"Mrs. Rogers?"

Jill stood up and my hand fell to the side. I stood beside her, eyeing the doc.

"I'm Mrs. Rogers." Her lips trembled and she ripped the tissue in her hands.

"He's out of surgery, Mrs. Rogers, and he's stable for now, but still in very critical condition."

She closed her eyes, as if offering a quick prayer, and my stomach left my throat, settling back down where it belonged.

"Can I see him?" she asked.

"Yes, but just for a few minutes. He's not out of the anesthetic yet, so he won't be able to see you or talk to you."

"I understand."

"Doctor, I'm Detective Contino, Dennis Police. When will I be able to talk to him?"

"I'm not sure, Detective. He's lost a lot of blood. He needs a lot of rest and we have to monitor his condition closely."

"Okay, I understand." Yeah, did I ever. Not too long ago, a doctor was saying something like that about me. "If you don't mind, I'd like to post a guard at his door all night."

"Certainly, Detective. Please notify our Chief of Security."

Jill Rogers looked at me and her lips creased slightly into a smile. "Thank you, Jack."

I gave the doc my card. "Please call me as soon as he is able to talk."

The doctor nodded and walked away, holding Jill Rogers by the arm.

I called headquarters to get a security detail for George Rogers before heading home. The call was brief, but I wasn't free yet. Coming across the waiting area carpet was Lynn Bradford.

"Okay, Jack, now's the time for you to fess up. Another violent attack has taken place and it will be another homicide if the victim doesn't make it. Was this the same guy, the one in the sketch you gave me? Come on, Jack. It'll come out eventually. Yes or no, the same guy?"

"Let's grab a seat, Lynn." I motioned to the sofa. In my high school football days, I learned that you had the other team as your opponent, but sometimes you also had the weather to deal with. In law enforcement, you have the good guys and you have the bad guys. But you also have the press working on you. They could be like bad weather.

"I told you I would honor your request not to print that sketch in the paper, but I can't hold back anymore. If it's the same guy, Jack, the people have a right to know."

"Look, I can't confirm that it's the same guy, but the description fits."

"Oh, for crying out loud, Jack, don't pussy foot around."

"Nobody saw his face except George Rogers and he can't talk right now, so I don't want you running a story that sends the people into a panic. It might be the same guy, but we honestly don't know that for sure. We'll have to get a description from George when he can talk."

"And what if he doesn't make it, Jack, then what?"

"He's stabilized, so the odds are in his favor. His wife is with him now. The doc is going to call me as soon as George is awake."

"I've got to run a story about this, Jack. It's my job. You can't keep this bottled up forever."

"So run your story, but please, don't start any CRAZED KILLER ON THE LOOSE stuff. Just print the facts, no wild speculation, please."

"It wouldn't be wild speculation, Jack. Three other people have been killed recently by a tall, heavy set guy wearing a dark hoodie. Whether the face matches the sketch really doesn't matter that much. This is looking like one guy to me and it will look that way to our readers, too. That's a fact."

She was right about that. If I put myself into civilian shoes, I'd reach the same conclusion. I looked down at my feet, but all I could see were cop shoes.

We were silent for a few seconds, but it felt like an hour.

"Jack, I understand your position. I really do, but you have to appreciate my situation, too. All right, here's what I'll do. I'll write the *Times* story about the attack, but I won't make any reference to the other killings, since this victim is still alive. I'll just describe him as a tall, heavy set guy, but I won't mention his clothes. But if the readers start putting two and two together, they'll start asking questions and I'll be sending them to you."

She had me. I couldn't stop her from writing about the attack and I'd have to trust her not to try to connect this one with the others.

"Very well, Lynn, I guess that's fair enough."

"Thanks, Jack. I'll let you see the story tonight if you like."

"Really? How long?"

"You'll have it in about two, maybe three hours. I'll drop it off at your house."

"You don't have my address."

"Don't be cute, Jack. Give me a break."

I slipped a card from my wallet and jotted my address on the back. "This won't make any points for you with Natalie, coming by my house late on a Sunday."

"Hey, it's not like I can send you a printed copy over the phone or something. It's this way or no way."

"Yeah, I guess."

After the guard detail arrived, I went home and told Nat what had happened and to expect the reporter to be stopping by. She was very understanding about the whole thing and very quiet, too quiet. She barely spoke to me for the rest of the evening.

I struggled in my mind to see this from her point of view. How could it be any different than mine? We had a great evening together and it was interrupted by the requirements of my occupation. What else could it look like and why would it piss her off so much?

Later, when Lynn Bradford rang the doorbell, she broke her silence. "Oh, Love 'em and Leave 'em Contino, your package has arrived."

Lynn Bradford kept her word. There was no mention of the sketch and no speculation that the attack on George Rogers was connected to the previous killings. Nonetheless, I wondered how long it would take for the public to start asking questions.

Chapter Twenty-Eight

"Ready, red, rock, one, set. One-TWO-three-FOUR-five . . ." On *Four* eleven players sprang into action, responding to the play the quarterback called at the line of scrimmage. They started from the old T-formation in the backfield, a remnant from the days of Red Grange. The right end blocked in, enveloping the defender aligned with his left shoulder. The right tackle threw himself at the defensive tackle opposite him, pushing him slightly to the left. The right guard pulled out of his position and ran full speed to his right, parallel to the line of scrimmage. He had no specific defender as a target. His mission was to seek and destroy the first opponent he saw.

The quarterback took the snap from center and spun back on his right heel, turning his back on the pulling guard, taking two steps into his backfield and deftly sliding the football against the gut of the left halfback, whose two hands closed around the ball, his right hand from below it and the other from the top. He followed his right halfback, who ran with careful body control toward the outside linebacker. The fullback rushed forward, filling the hole created by the pulling guard and crashing into the bigger defender trying to find the football. The ball carrier ran at three-quarter speed until his blocker did his job, creating the opportunity which signaled the runner to accelerate to full speed, cut behind the block and race up the field for seven yards before defenders caught him from both sides, one paying the price for being there first, as his head was snapped back by the ball carrier's straight arm to his helmet.

Tommy Shea stood along the sidelines, a dark raincoat protecting him from the dampness. He clapped his hands in reply to the action on the field. He loved the way football went from a moment of silence, eleven men facing eleven men, and then erupted into motion, accented by the sound of pads cracking into one another. The coach's whistle blew repeatedly, a sharp staccato, calling the end of all action.

The Tufts University football practice field was in Medford, not far from Shea's home area in Somerville, the Winter Hill section. He enjoyed watching the young men practice the rugged game, punishing their bodies, trying to best the other guy. Man-to-man pushed Shea's hot buttons.

But Tommy Shea seldom went one-on-one anymore. He'd take on anybody, all right, but he always had help waiting in the wings. He made that decision many years ago after a fight outside a Somerville bar went the wrong way for him. He got in a good one on his big opponent, Jack Contino, the wop cop, as Shea liked to call him. A shard of glass hidden in his pocket gave him a weapon to even the odds, as he saw it, and he cut Contino across the chin. But a crashing blow from Contino's big hand put Tommy's lights out. Getting even was a life's mission. Revenge could come in many ways, so a life of crime gave him many opportunities to get under the cop's skin.

Shea never turned to look at the stocky guy lumbering across the field from the roadside parking area, his hands thrust into his jacket pockets. The guy had on old khaki pants, a blue T-shirt and a shiny nylon jacket that said Red Sox across the front. A blue hat with a big red B on it completed the sports fan look.

"I hope we had a good weekend, Jimmy. You've been in a slump lately," said Shea, his eyes on the football team.

The stocky guy pulled up beside Shea. "Tufts is looking pretty good this year, huh, Tommy?"

"I'm not worried about Tufts, Jimmy boy. I'm more concerned with you. How'd you do this weekend?"

"The slump's over, Tommy. My guys did real good. They came through in the clutch. Good clutch hitters, my boys." Jimmy's hands came out of the jacket pockets and he pulled at each side of his garment, popping open a few buttons. He reached inside and extracted a white envelope, bulging with the contents. He slipped it to Tommy Shea quickly, standing close to him, almost belly-to-belly, to block the transaction from curious eyes. Since they were alone on the sidelines, their privacy was secure.

Shea took the envelope and stuffed it into his coat pocket. "I trust this is going to make me happy, Jimbo."

"It's going to make you real happy, Boss, real happy."

"How happy is that, Jimmy?"

"About four-grand happy. Like I said, my boys played the right teams this week, so the pool paid off real good. Of course, sometimes you got to persuade a guy that his luck could be a lot worse, so he dug into his own pocket after I slapped him around a little bit, just for his own good, you see."

"You're an old pro, Jimmy boy. You understand how this works. It's better to be the guy who does the slapping, than the other way around, yes?"

"Yes, indeed, Boss." Jimmy's voice cracked as he spoke and the smile left his face. He knew how Tommy could be if there was continued bad news about the weekly earnings. "You got anything else for me, Jimbo?"

"Anything else . . . oh, about that license plate. Yeah, I talked to our boy at the Registry. He ran it for me for his usual fee, of course, and he gave me the information. The guy lives on the Cape. Here it is."

Jimmy drew a slip of paper out of his pants pocket and handed it to Shea, their hands hanging by their sides, barely touching.

"Good. Nice work, Jimbo." Shea turned and strutted away. No further small talk was needed or wanted. Shea was curious about that guy from the Cape who bought a round of drinks for his group yesterday in Boston. He didn't like to be in the dark about people. Friendly gestures didn't always come from friends.

When Shea reached his car, he eased himself into the driver's seat and closed the door. He pulled the piece of paper out of his pocket and glared at it. He paused for a moment, trying to recall the name but nothing surfaced in his mind. . The name and address of the owner of the Chevy Nova meant nothing to him. He folded the paper and dropped it into his shirt pocket, found his keys in his coat and started the engine. It was a good day for a drive to the Cape.

Shea pulled off his raincoat and tossed it onto the passenger seat. There was always some traffic in mid-afternoon on Rte. 128, even though it wasn't rush hour yet, especially at the Braintree split, where the Southeast Expressway connected to the highway. Lane shifters, some going north, some going south, caused the slowdown. Shea was in no hurry. He kept his vehicle to the right at the split and emerged from the slow traffic onto Rte. 3 south.

It was nearly five o'clock when Shea reached Hyannis and located the address written on the piece of paper in his pocket. It was an old, white clapboard-sided house with pale blue shutters, situated on a corner near the intersection of Main Street and Lewis Bay Road. He parked across the street in a small lot outside a liquor store, his car facing the old house.

Shea sat patiently in his auto, watching the house across the street. A dark Chevy Nova was one of three cars parked on the sandy soil beside the house. Shea pulled a pair of small binoculars from his glove compartment. They gave him a clear view of the Nova's license plate. The number matched the one he had on paper.

As boredom crept into Shea, he left the friendly confines of his car and sauntered into the liquor store to grab a cold six pack of beer. There was a newspaper rack near the checkout, so he decided to grab the local daily to see if there was anything of interest to him happening on Cape Cod. Halfway down the front page a headline got his attention. BARTENDER STABBED OUTSIDE SAND DUNE.

Shea eased himself back behind the wheel, popped a can of beer and read the article about the stabbing. It described a tall, heavy-set guy as a possible suspect and a dark-colored, old car as his vehicle, as seen by a witness. Shea dropped the paper and stared at the old Nova across the street. The guy who bought the drinks for him was tall and heavy, but these things could be a coincidence, not proof that the guy was involved with the stabbing.

Tommy was well into his second beer when he saw the husky guy come out of the building and approach the dark Nova. The guy went to the passenger side of the car, opened the door and leaned in to get something from the glove compartment. Shea got a clear look through his binoculars. His memory was triggered by the guy's build and clothes, blue jeans, dark hooded sweatshirt and sneakers.

Shea couldn't place the guy. He had no memory of him or his vehicle. *Why did this guy come all the way to Boston, pay for play with Ginny and buy me a drink, all the time keeping his distance and not making an introduction?* Tommy grabbed the door handle and started to push it open, planning on confronting the stranger head on. But he decided that might be the wrong approach, so he stayed in his car. *Better to keep an eye on this guy and see what his game is.* Shea drove home, all the while sorting out options for dealing with this new challenge.

Chapter Twenty-Nine

It was early Wednesday morning when Leo called me at my office. I figured it was about Billy D'Agostino's funeral.

"Hello, Leo, what's the day and time on the service?"

"Greetings and salutations, to you, too, old pal. It's tomorrow at ten, but that's not why I called."

"If you're trying to mooch a free meal, come on down this weekend."

"Not a bad idea, Jack. Will do, soon, but I'll have to take a rain check this weekend. I've got a hot date with a chick from Newton. She's a vice principal at the high school, a real authority figure, just my type."

"I don't think you have a type, pal."

"Sure I do. It's the gal I'm with at the moment. That's my type. But that's not what I'm talking about. I've got some news about D'Agostino that might interest you."

"I'm listening, Leo."

"The word from one of Billy's associates is that he didn't own that cottage by the sea just for pleasure. I told you he had his own boat dock and a yacht there. I have good word that he was running drugs out of the house. His suppliers would bring them in on his yacht, which had a tendency to change its size and appearance from time-to-time. Different boats for different shipments."

"Well, I'll be. Has the FBI heard about this?"

"Oh, yeah. I told our old contact, Agent Nelson, this morning and he said he's sending a team down there immediately to search the place. He said to pass this on to you in an official capacity. He said you're welcome to visit the scene, but don't bring an army with you. His guys will take care of it."

"Frankly, they can have it, but I'll go check in with him anyway."

"Jack, there's another thing. Word has it that Billy didn't own that house alone. You might want to check out the deed. The talkative associate says Tommy Shea is part owner, kind of a silent partner."

"Hmmm, that makes sense. Billy wasn't the type to run a drug operation by himself. He'd need big time help, so it wouldn't surprise me to see Shea's name on the deed. That way, if something happened to Billy, and I guess it did, then Shea just keeps the operation for himself and owns some choice waterfront property to boot."

"But Jack, if the Feds find drugs anywhere around the place, Shea's in for some trouble."

"Which is why I'm betting that Agent Nelson and his crew will come up dry on this one. Shea's boys must have swept the place clean by now. Something must have gone wrong in his deal with Billy and Shea decided to render the deal null and void, in his special way. But Billy was killed in Boston, so that's out of my jurisdiction. I've got other troubles to worry about."

"Jack, I don't like the fact that Shea's business has spread to your town. There could be a reason for that. And this possible serial killer could be more than meets the eye."

"You think there's a connection?"

"I don't know, Jack, but stranger things have happened. I think I'll keep an eye on Shea for a while, in case he's headed down Rte. 3."

"I doubt that, since his house is of interest to the FBI now. But watch what he's doing at home. See if there are any new players showing up on his team and keep your distance."

"No problem, Jacko, I'll use some of my part-timers to bird dog the guy."

"Good. Give me the address for Billy's house, will you? And, be nice with that Assistant Principal. You don't want to wind up in detention. It will go on your permanent record, maybe haunt you forever."

"Like I said, Jack, she's my kind of authority figure."

I got the address from Leo and drove over to meet up with the Feds. It was a small, nice-looking house on Harbor Way on the Bass River in West Dennis. There were several short streets in a row along the shore, each with small cottages and boat docks. A couple of black Crown Vics were parked outside. Two dark suited agents were outside scouring the grounds and the dock. One approached me as I got out of my Dennis Police car.

"I'm Jack Contino," I said as I flashed my badge at the man.

"You must be looking for Agent Nelson. He said to watch for you. He's inside."

Nelson was standing in the living room, his hands on his hips, watching as his team searched the place. He turned from side to side, as if he were conducting an orchestra, only without the wand.

"Nice to see you, Jack," he said without looking right at me.

"And a good day to you, too, Agent Nelson. So, you think Billy D. ran a drug business here?"

"That's the tip we got from your man Leo. He also said the word has it that Tommy Shea might be involved in this, that he's co-owner of the place. You want to check out the deed for us? We don't want an FBI presence to alarm anyone at the court house."

"No problem. I was planning on doing that. I'd be curious to know if Shea is opening up shop in Dennis, but I hope not. I've got enough trouble of my own here and I don't want to hear that Shea's getting anything going in Dennis."

I gave Agent Nelson a quick rundown on the murders I was investigating.

"Wow, you sure have got your hands full. Well, if anything pops up in this place, I'll let you know, but we'll take care of it. Just let me know whose names are on that deed."

"Will do," I said. "How's it going?"

"Nothing so far," said Nelson. "Looks like a clean house. I thought there was supposed to be a boat?"

"From what Leo said, there are a lot of boats, coming and going," I replied.

Agent Nelson looked around. "We'll contact the owners of these other cottages and see if they can tell us anything."

I nodded. "Leo's going to keep an eye on Shea and his buddies up north. He thinks that there might be a connection between Shea and what's been going on here. I don't think so, though. But I suppose there's no harm in keeping an eye open."

"Hmm. Off hand, I can't think of any way those murders could be part of Shea's operation, unless he's got a freelancer on his hands. Maybe one of his boys is going rogue on him. Oh, and tell Barbado to check in with me if he's going to be bird-dogging Shea. I don't want him getting in the way of my boys. We're going to be keeping tabs on Shea for a while, ourselves."

"No problem, Agent Nelson. Leo's no rookie. He knows the drill. You know, going rogue on Shea is a dangerous thing to do. I still don't see anything that could connect them. There's no sign of big money involved, just senseless killings. Hard to figure. Well, it's been nice, Agent Nelson. Time to go check out the deed on this fine place."

Chapter Thirty

Tommy Shea was mad as hell. He pounded his fist on the desk in Joe Vito's office at Club 77.

"Hey, take it easy, will you?" said Joe. "We'll get to the bottom of this."

"You're damned right we will and somebody's going to get to the bottom of the ocean before it's over with. There's another rat in the organization and this cat's going to catch his ass." Shea poured himself a shot of whiskey from the bottle on the desk in front of him and knocked it down.

"It's bad enough that D'Agostino was a rat," said Tommy. "So we fix him. So how come the Feds show up at the Cape house in Dennis after Billy's taken care of?"

Joe Vito swung from side to side in his swivel chair at his desk. "I wish I knew. It's crazy. Who would be dumb enough to do that, especially after seeing what happens to rats like Billy D. Tom, you got to look hard at all your boys. Anybody acting funny lately, maybe somebody with an axe to grind against you? Maybe somebody new?"

"My boys! What the fuck makes you think it's one of MY boys? Maybe it's one of your crew. There's always been a little edginess from some of your guys since we made this business deal."

"I know. I know. Wops and Micks don't mix too well, as some like to say. Hey, that's horseshit. Business is business and everybody makes out when we score. Yeah, okay, I got to look at my guys, too. I mean, it's somebody, right? But who?"

Shea rose up from his chair and paced the floor, his glass still in his hand. His left hand slapped at his leg. "Let's see. What about that bartender of yours? He's been around a long time with you and maybe he doesn't like his position so much anymore. Maybe he wants something extra, like a nice chunk from the Feds and protection in case something doesn't work right. Maybe him."

"Big Ted? Not a chance. He's been with me a long time all right, which is why I know he's okay. The guy's loyal as hell. No way he's a rat."

Shea shook his head, like the light bulb on a bright idea just went dim. "Naw, it's not him. Got to be somebody new, except I haven't taken in anybody new for a while."

"Me neither. Unless one of my guys brought somebody in and hasn't told me about it yet. But he'd be too low-level to know anything useful to the Feds. I'm stumped."

Tommy poured another whiskey, but this time he just took a sip, as if he didn't want to lose his concentration. He paced some more.

"Joe, what if, just what if, it's not a guy inside the organization?"

"What the hell does that mean? How would a guy outside know anything? That's nuts."

"Maybe not. What if it's a guy who hangs out here now and then and has big ears? What if it's somebody who likes to shoot the breeze with people, like a *bartender*, to get information. And maybe this guy takes a turn with one of the girls and gets her to jab a lot. He gets some stuff here, some stuff there, maybe he adds it all up, thinks he's got something and brings it to the Feds. Maybe it's somebody like that."

Joe leaned forward in his chair and leaned his elbows on the desk. His eyes opened wide. "You know somebody like that, Tommy?"

"No, not really, but maybe I do."

"What the fuck, Shea. Make sense, will you?"

Shea took another sip of whiskey. He paced some more, nodding his head, liking his own idea the more he thought about it.

"Joe, there was a guy in here a few days ago, last Sunday afternoon. He sat at the bar for a while, then Big Ted set him up with Ginny. See what I mean. He talks to Big Ted for a while, then he spends time with Ginny in the back room. He could squeeze out information that way, a little at a time."

"Tommy, lots of guys could fall into that picture. Bartenders talk to customers. It's what they do, besides mixing drinks. And as for Ginny, she's a good gal. Besides, how much talking can she do when she's working her mouth the other way? Be real."

"Yeah, but maybe this guy's different. After he finished with Ginny, he comes back to the bar and sets up me and my guys with a round of drinks. Then, bold as brass, he walks right by our table on the way out and gives me a wave, like he knows me, for Chrissakes. It all caught me off guard, but I had Bobby chase after him. Bobby got the make and license plate on his car and I checked him out. He lives on the Cape. How's that for a coincidence, Joey boy? And before you know it, the Feds are at the house in Dennis. I don't like it."

"Wait, Tommy, just wait. Let's not jump to conclusions. I don't like that picture, either, but it still doesn't seem right. What could Ted or Ginny know about Billy D?"

"Maybe we underestimate what they know. Maybe they take in information as well as give it out, without really meaning to, you know?"

Joe Vito sat straight up in his chair, like he'd been hit by a bolt of electricity. "Geeze, Shea, you could be right. I guess we all run off at the mouth, now and then, especially when we're among friends, including drinking buddies and good-time girls. Maybe we should talk to Ginny and Big Ted. Got to be sly with Ted, though. If we're wrong, we don't want to make him think we doubt his loyalty. That could give him reason to turn on us later. I like Ginny, but she can be replaced if need be."

"Hey, maybe your bartender is loyal to you, but I don't have any reason to treat him with kid gloves," said Tommy.

"Look, Shea, don't try shaking him down. I'll find out what he knew about Billy D. If I find out that he's a weak link, I'll take care of him. You check out Ginny, if you want."

Shea broke into a grin. "Oh, I'll check her out all right. Count on it. And I'll check out this guy from the Cape."

"That's fine. And don't forget Contino. With the Feds in the picture, he won't be far away."

"Oh, Contino is always on my radar. Don't worry about that. Right now, I think I'll pay Ginny a visit. I'm sure I can get something helpful out of her."

Joe Vito swallowed hard.

Shea left the office and strolled out to the main room to find Ginny. It didn't take a lot of searching. She was at the bar talking to Big Ted. It was a routine sight, but one that now put a sour taste in Shea's mouth.

His mood switched from suspicion to lust as he eyed Ginny, standing at the bar in black fish net tights and G-string. She had a sheer white blouse draped on her back, leaving her full breasts with pasties exposed. Her right hand caressed a water glass in front of her and her left hand supported her chin.

She didn't flinch when Tommy Shea grabbed her right buttock and gave it a firm squeeze. Management and employees were always grabbing her ass. But if a customer did it, he might not be able to use his hand for a few weeks.

Big Ted had his arms out to each side, palms down on the bar, but he broke off his conversation with Ginny when Shea arrived.

"What can I get you, Tommy?" asked Ted.

"I'm good for now, big guy. I just need to have a little time with Ginny."

Ginny straightened up. "Why, Tommy, it's been a long time. To what do I owe the pleasure?"

Shea just looked at her, his tongue brushing the inside of his lower teeth. He nodded in the direction of the back rooms and walked that way. Ginny gave a glance at Big Ted as she followed Shea.

They went into a room directly opposite Joe Vito's office. It was the room Ginny often used to entertain special guests and paying customers, like a guy in a hooded sweatshirt.

Shea held the door open for Ginny and motioned her into the room. She instinctively went to the large sofa in back. Shea closed and locked the door.

"Well, Tommy boy, what's your pleasure?" She dropped her blouse onto the sofa and then peeled off her pasties, tossing them onto her blouse.

"You're on the right track, girl. Just keep stripping," said Shea.

Ginny obeyed and peeled off the rest. She turned to face Shea, presenting her naked self to him, her lips pursed in a grin, her back to the door. She closed her eyes as his hands caressed her breasts.

"You take good care of your body, Ginny girl," said Tommy.

"Dancing is hard work, Tommy, a good workout every day. It keeps the goods firm and tight, from head to toe. I'm glad you like the package."

"Yeah, it's quite a nice package, Ginny." He ran his hands down her front and then moved to her back. His finger traced her spine and he spread his hand out when he reached her ass, caressing both buttocks. Now his finger caressed her crack.

"Oh, so you want a little back door action. Ah, well, if that's what you want, Tommy, sure. There are condoms in the table drawer. I hope there's some Vaseline there, too." She forced a laugh. "Say, don't you want me to help you undress?" She groped at his belt and he slapped her hand away.

"Don't move unless I tell you."

"Sure, sure, Tommy, I just thought . . ."

"Don't think, Ginny. Just listen. How would you describe your position right now?" Shea ran a finger down her spine.

"I guess you would say I'm open for business," she answered, her voice quivering.

"That's right, your ass is there for the taking and I can take it any way I want. I can give it to you in a way you'll never forget."

Ginny's breathing became labored. "I . . . I don't understand, Tommy. Is something wrong? I'll please you anytime you want."

"Yes you will, Ginny girl. Yes you will. I just hope you never displease me."

"What do you mean, Tommy? I would never do anything to displease you. You know that. Really."

Shea circled her, a finger in constant contact.

"Well, Ginny girl, I'll tell you what would *displease* me. If you talk too much to somebody I don't like, like a Fed or a cop or somebody who works with them, that would displease me very much."

"What, Tommy, talk to a Fed or a cop? That's crazy. You know I'd never do that. Never."

"What about that guy last Sunday? What did you talk to him about?"

"Tommy, I already told you, that was just a John. We didn't talk. I couldn't, remember, I had a mouthful."

Shea slapped her ass hard. "Don't get cute with me, Ginny."

"I'm sorry, Tommy. I just meant that, well, you know, I was busy ... working on him. We didn't talk about anything but how he wanted it, you know."

"What about Billy D? Did you ever talk about him?"

"Billy D? Tommy, I never heard of Billy D. Who's that?"

"You never heard of Billy D'Agostino?"

"D'Agostino. That sounds familiar. I think I've heard that name. You know how you sometimes overhear talk at the bar and such. But I don't know anything about him. Maybe I heard Big Ted mention that name. I don't know."

Shea stood behind Ginny. He ran his hands down her sides and let a thumb prod her. She gasped.

"Okay, Ginny. I believe you. Now, just remember the position you're in. You're naked. You've got nothing and your ass is mine. Got it?"

"Yeah, yeah, I got it. Really, Tommy, I'd never do anything like that. Never."

"Okay, sweet cheeks. You're good stuff. I don't know another chick as cool as you."

At first Ginny didn't move, her back still to the door, worried what Shea's next move might be. But as his voice trailed off and she heard the door open and close, she relaxed knowing he was gone, but still wondered about his next move.

Chapter Thirty-One

The white haired lady was there as always, working diligently for the people of Barnstable County at the Registry of Deeds. Her world was so orderly. Her work environment was quiet and peaceful. People came in and she helped them find what they needed. Research a deed. Go to the conference room for a real estate closing. All day, every day, just help others in a calm, sedate atmosphere and go home at five o'clock. Neat and tidy work, day in and day out for thirty years. I could tell by the look on her face that she relished her work. It suited her perfectly. I hope she appreciated what she had. I'd bet she did. I'd bet my life on it.

Do your homework. That's what people say. Be thorough in your job and dig deep. Well, this was my homework and I was going to school again. I learned that Tommy Shea's name was on the deed with Billy D'Agostino for the house at Bass River. But there was a third name, too. There it was, Giuseppe Vitigliano, aka Joe Vito. What a pair.

Joe Vito, Boston Mafia boss, owner of Club 77, other establishments in the city and all-around scumbag. I knew that Shea would frequent Club 77, but I never figured he and Vito would go into business together. Their blood didn't mix well.

When I got back to Billy D's house, Agent Nelson and his team were finishing up.

"This isn't what I expected, but it sure is interesting," said Agent Nelson. "Tommy Shea and Joe Vito doing business together, mixing their money. Wow."

"Unfortunately, it doesn't prove anything criminal was going on here, at least not proof we can take to court, not yet," I said. "But we know these guys weren't setting up a Boy Scout camp."

"Don't worry, Jack. We'll get them. It's just a matter of time."

"It's just a matter of FBI time. Leo's going to have to be my bird dog. I've got my hands full with some homicides right now." Did I ever.

"Any chance this is connected to the psycho you are chasing on the Cape, Jack?"

"The murders are all different, but they seem to be the work of one man, some chubby creep who wears a pair of jeans, sneakers and a dark, hooded sweatshirt. But here's the kicker. He attacked a bartender, George Rogers. You remember him?"

"Yeah, sure do. His testimony put Sidney Fish away for us. You think your psycho attacked him? Why?"

"Don't know why. But a waitress at the place said she heard the guy yell something about Tommy Shea when he was stabbing George out back of the place."

Agent Nelson took a deep breath and let it out slowly. "Why would a crazy killer be linked with Tommy Shea? That doesn't figure. Well, we're going to keep surveillance on this place to see if anything happens."

I wiped my forehead with a finger. "Vito and Shea have always been real good at covering their tracks, so I don't think they'll do anything obvious. I wouldn't be surprised to see a FOR SALE sign go up on this place, now that they know the Bureau is watching."

"True, Jack, but for every action there is a reaction. We just have to watch closely for it. It might be here or it might be in Boston or Somerville. Go find your killer, Jack, and watch out for that connection to Shea."

I'll get that hoodie whacko, for sure. And my antennae are always checking for Shea. Always.

I was in my car and about to drive back to police headquarters when a radio call came through for me. The dispatcher said I was to go directly to Cape Cod Hospital. George Rogers was awake.

I didn't like having to bother a wounded man in a hospital bed, but I had to talk to him.

When I got there, I identified myself at the desk and made my way to his room. I nodded at the guard we had posted outside the room. Inside, Jill Rogers was at her husband's bedside, clutching his hand. She turned to look at me as I entered the room and her face changed from joy to something less than that.

"Hello, Detective," she said. She turned back to her husband. I guess I wouldn't be too happy to see me, either.

George looked up at me and made a wrinkled expression, as if he was trying to acknowledge my presence. He looked awful. He was ghostly pale and had an oxygen tube in his nose and an I-V feed in the back of his right hand.

"Hello, Jill. George, I'm real sorry about this. I'm glad you're doing better. I promise not to take long, but you know that I have to talk to you if we're going to catch this guy."

George nodded while Jill still held his left hand with both of hers. I recalled the expression, "A penny for your thoughts." Any thoughts Jill had about me right now weren't worth a penny.

I was carrying a manila envelope with me. From it, I extracted the sketch of our suspect in the homicides and showed it to George. "George, do you recognize this guy?"

George examined the sketch for a long moment as I held it up in front of him. He peered at it, squinting as if the room light caused a glare on the paper. I brought it a little closer to his face. He looked at me and nodded affirmatively.

"Good, George, that's great. Can you tell me where you recognize him from?"

Before he could answer, George reached for the cup of water that was on the tray to his right. It was a plastic cup with a lid and a straw protruding through it. He took a sip.

"From the bar," he said. "He was at the bar."

"George, do you mean that he was at the bar on the night you were attacked?" He nodded again.

"George, was he the man who attacked you? Can you tell me that?"

He shook his head then took another sip of water. "It happened so fast. I didn't get a good look at the guy. Too fast, too much pain."

"Good, that's very good, George. I won't take any more of your time. I'll check back tomorrow to see how you're doing. Thanks for your help. Thank you, Jill."

Jill Rogers nodded as I left the room. Her expression didn't change.

It wasn't much, but this information confirmed our suspicions. The guy who attacked George was the same guy committing the random murders and he was connected or involved with Tommy Shea, somehow. But how? We needed proof.

Chapter Thirty-Two

I started the day with two shots of bourbon at breakfast, but at the office it was coffee time. It was mid-morning when I got a call from Leo. "Good morning, Officer Krupke, how goes it in Dennis?"

"You're not going to break out into song now, are you?"

"Okay, how about I sing the news to you? Here's a number from the Boston *Trib*. *Hey everybody there are killings on the Cape, multiple bodies and just one suspect.*"

"Whoa, give me that without the sing song, Leo." I held my coffee cup just away from my mouth, ready to take a gulp.

"There's an article in this morning's *Trib* about the murders on the Cape and the writer describes one suspect, a big, heavyset guy with a hooded sweatshirt and blue jeans. The reporter is named Lynn Bradford."

"Yeah, I know her. She writes for the Cape Cod *Times*. I guess she also writes for the *Trib*. She let me see her story before the paper was going to run it."

"You mean you okay'd this, even the part about Tommy Shea?"

I put my cup down on the desk. "What? There isn't anything about Shea."

"Oh yes there is. She talks about the attack on George Rogers and later says that there may be a link to *famed Boston area mob figure Tommy Shea*. She says his name was mentioned by a witness because she heard someone call it out loud when Rogers was being assaulted. What gives, Jack?"

"I don't know, but I'm going to find out. I never said anything to her about Shea's name being called. She said she wouldn't even mention the other murders, just write about the attack on Rogers. I'll have to check the Cape Cod *Times*. Hold on, Leo. Sgt. Pearson's waving to me. He's got a copy."

I went to Jim's desk and scanned the front page of the *Times* that was there. After checking out the article, I went back to my call with Leo.

"Her story in the *Times* is the one she showed to me. She must have decided to pull a fast one, writing a very different story for the Boston paper."

"They sell the *Trib* on the Cape, do they not? She knows that, doesn't she?"

"Oh, she knows that, all right. I guess she thought she was being clever. I'm going to have to have a little chat with Ms. Bradford. I don't know how she found out about Shea's name being heard by a witness, unless she went directly to the waitress. She kept that little bit of information from me. She knows I didn't want anything being printed that could cause a panic. People are going to think we have a maniac running loose, one connected to the Boston Mob. That's just great."

I was boiling mad, but stopped myself from saying anything out loud to Leo about what I'd like to do to Lynn Bradford. I shook my head and grabbed some deep breaths.

"You okay, old buddy?" asked Leo. "Haven't punched a hole in the desk yet, have you?"

"No, no, I'm fine, Leo. Listen, thanks for catching this. It certainly changes my day's schedule. Visiting Ms. Bradford is now first on my list of things to do."

"Don't do anything I wouldn't do under the circumstances," said Leo.

"Don't worry, old pal, I'll bring an officer along with me . . . for protection. Let me know if you have any more surprises." I hung up and took a deep breath, then called for Officer Orlando. I figured having a female officer with me would help me keep my cool.

We took a squad car to the *Times* office in Hyannis. I let Orlando drive, giving me some time to calm down as a passenger. It was only a few miles, but it seemed to take forever. I passed the time by tapping my knee, rubbing my palms and cracking my knuckles.

"Take it easy, Jack. We'll get there soon enough," said Orlando. "I don't think I've ever seen you get this steamed up."

I glanced over at her and then looked at my hands. I folded them together and held them on my lap. Maybe I should have sat on them. "Okay, Officer, I'm calming down now, see."

"Does Tommy Shea read the newspaper? Maybe he won't even see it."

"He reads the papers, all right. He may be a whack-job sociopath, but he's not stupid. He keeps up on the news, just in case he's in it. He likes seeing his name in print, but he might not like it this time, since the story suggests a link to him with the George Rogers attack. Knowing Shea, I figure he might make some kind of a move on this."

"Maybe that's good, Jack, right? If he is connected to this hoodie guy, maybe it'll smoke him out, don't you think?"

The more I worked with Karen Orlando, the more I liked her. "You're catching on, kid. Yes, it could work out in our favor if it causes Shea to make a move. That just might happen. After all, he's not as calm about things as I am."

Orlando gave me a quick look, showing a tight smile. She was good medicine. I felt much calmer and in control.

We pulled into the *Times* parking lot at the intersection of Main Street and Barnstable Road. It was a stone's throw from the Ocean Street docks, where pleasure craft, fishing boats and island ferries populated the area. Not a bad place to go to work every day. To that extent, I envied Lynn Bradford. I took a deep breath as we got out of the squad car. The ocean air filled my lungs. Orlando still had that grin on her face.

"Hey, kid, I didn't get this in Boston. You're living in a good spot for police work. There are much worse, believe me." She nodded and grinned some more.

The building was an expansive one-story brick, with wide, white trim and a pointed arch over the front door with the name *Cape Cod Times* above it in large letters. We made our entrance, got directions to Bradford's office and strolled down a long hallway of private offices. It was in sharp contrast to the Boston *Tribune*, where all the reporters had desks crammed together in a large, open room. Whenever I was there over the years, I felt like I was in a cafeteria converted into work space. This was typical Cape Cod quaint.

We found an office with her name plate beside the door, which was open. Lynn Bradford was sitting behind her desk reading something, a handful of papers in her grip. She looked up as we entered.

"Good morning, Detective, Officer. To what do I owe the pleasure?" Was she real cool or just dumb? I never thought she was dumb.

"Good morning to you, Ms. Bradford. See how modern I am, you know, with the Ms. Stuff and all. Just a sec, okay?"

I motioned for Karen Orlando to move into the room and I closed the door behind her. I walked up close to the desk.

"I THOUGHT WE HAD A DEAL. Damn you, Bradford. What the fa . . . hell do you think you're doing, writing one article for the *Times* and another one for the Boston *Trib?*"

"Calm down, Detective, calm down."

"Calm down? You try to incite panic in the streets and you want me to calm down. That's rich. I thought you were a reporter I could trust. So much for that."

"Look, Jack, I gave you my word in good faith."

"Oh, sure you did. Then how come you wrote that article talking about the guy calling out the name Tommy Shea, famed Boston area Mob figure, I believe you called him?"

"Look, after I gave you the story, I kept working. I went to the Sand Dune to talk to anybody who might be helpful. I found the waitress that you talked to and she told me the whole story. The part about Shea made this story too big to ignore, Detective. It's NEWS and I have a right to report it, hell, a duty. If this hoodie guy is tied to Tommy Shea and the other killings, I can't hold back. The game was changed."

"Why didn't you at least have the integrity to call me before you wrote that story?" I was still steaming.

"Jack, it was three o'clock in the morning by the time I'd written that piece. There was no time. I had a job to do and, hell, I barely made deadline. I had to dictate the whole thing over the phone."

The office door burst open and a gray-haired, short guy came in. With gray slacks, a white shirt with sleeves rolled up and a loosened necktie, he looked like he was doing a Perry White impression from Superman. "Is everything okay in here, Lynn? Should I call the police?"

He didn't notice the uniformed Officer Orlando who was shielded by the door. When she stepped out into view, fighting off that grin, Perry White's jaw dropped. "Oh, I didn't see you there, Officer. Say, just what's going on here? They can hear you almost out to the lobby."

I inched closer to him and held up my shield. "I'm Chief Detective Contino, Dennis Police and this is Officer Orlando. We're having a discussion with Ms. Bradford." I arched over him. "Would you please excuse us so that we can continue? We'll hold down the noise."

Perry White stepped back through the door. "Oh, yes, of course. You are the police. Good, then. I guess everything is under control. Carry on, Bradford."

I closed the door as he left.

Lynn Bradford was first to speak after White left. "As I said, Jack, I never intended to violate my word to you. I meant what I said. I filed that story, as you saw it, with the *Times*. But you know I also write occasional stories as a stringer for the *Tribune*. I had news under my belt, big news, and it had to be told. It's my job, Jack."

"Well, your job might have serious consequences. Tommy Shea is nobody to fool with. He's been known to make people disappear if they piss him off. Do you understand me?"

If Lynn had been thinking of giving me the First Amendment speech, she thought better of it. She looked like a puppy dog who had been scolded for barking.

"I'm sorry, Jack. I never meant to violate your trust. We both have tough jobs to do and we have to do them. Really, Jack, I'm sorry."

The contrition in her voice was genuine. I was beginning to feel sorry for her, rather than angry at her. She could have put herself in harm's way.

"Apology accepted, Lynn." That's all I wanted to say. No lecture needed. I turned, opened the door and left. Karen Orlando followed without speaking, all the way to the car. When we got there, I started for the driver's door, but Orlando cut me off.

"I've got it, Jack."

"Oh, yeah, sure. I wasn't thinking."

"You're thinking about something, Jack."

"I'm thinking about what might happen next. Her story could be a trigger point."

Chapter Thirty-Three

He pulled his old Nova into the small parking lot at *Nell and Jed's* restaurant and backed it into a small spot away from other cars. There were only a few sedans, a pick up and two electric company trucks. It was just before noon and the lunchtime patrons were starting to drift in. Nell and Jed's was a popular West Yarmouth establishment on Rte. 28 that overflowed during the summer season.

He sauntered in and took a seat at the end of the L-shaped counter located along the right side of the room. He took the last spot at the bottom end of the L. There were two empty stools to his left and the first three seats around the corner were occupied by an elderly couple and a husky guy with the uniform of the power company. The couple was eating club sandwiches, while the working man nursed a coffee and read the Boston *Tribune*.

An elderly waitress behind the counter approached him with a water pitcher.

"Hello, love," she said as she poured a glass of water for him and placed a menu on the counter. "Care for coffee or something else to drink?"

"No, water's fine. No need for the menu. I'll have the clam basket. I usually do when I come here. Thanks."

"Okay, love. Coming right up." She scribbled the order in her pad and walked away.

He tapped his fingers on the counter and sipped his water. The silence was broken by the working man. He folded the newspaper lengthwise, making it possible to read the story on the right side, bottom corner of page three. "Oh boy, looks like Boston bad guys are on the Cape," he said to nobody in particular. It got the attention of the elderly woman.

"What was that, young man? What do you mean?"

"There's a story here about a bartender being knifed recently in Dennis and a waitress told the reporter that she heard somebody yell the name Tommy Shea outside the building, apparently where the attack was happening. He's some big time Boston gangster, from what I hear and read. He's been implicated in a lot of crimes over the years, but they usually can't catch him."

"Pretty slippery, is he?" asked the older man, holding his sandwich with two hands.

"Apparently," answered the working man.

"Was the bartender killed?" asked the woman, grimacing.

"Hmm, doesn't say," said the worker, running his eyes up and down the paper. "Just says he was knifed. Says the bartender testified in a murder trial a while ago and the guy was convicted and is doing life in Walpole. But it says they don't think there is any connection between this attack and the trial. Says maybe the name Tommy Shea was shouted out as a distraction."

"Could be," said the older man. "But that's a heck of a coincidence, you know, the bartender being a witness in another trial and then getting stabbed. Sure sounds like revenge, if you ask me."

What the fuck. Somebody heard me, after all, a waitress with a big mouth. It wasn't Tommy Shea, you assholes. It was me. It was ME. I'm the talent here, local talent. That's me. Damn. That bar is full of big mouths. Maybe I need to shut that waitress up, too. Damn.

"Henry and I don't go out much anymore, at least not at night," said the woman. "What's the name of that place where it happened?"

"Ah . . . the Sand Dune, in Dennis."

"Oh, my goodness, we used to go there a lot, years ago," said the woman. "The owner plays the piano, sings and tells dirty jokes. We love the dirty jokes. He's so funny. He's older than us, I think."

The working man stared at the woman for a second and shook his head, turning back to his newspaper.

The waitress brought the clam basket out. "Is it getting cold outside?" she asked. "You look all bundled up in that sweatshirt, hood up around your head and all."

"I didn't notice. I guess so. I'm comfortable like this. That's all."

He poked his fork at the clams as if he couldn't decide which one to take first. Multiple targets required planning. He settled on the one on top of the pile, thrusting his fork into the belly, dabbing it into the paper cup of tartar sauce, lifting it and pulling it off the fork with his mouth. He repeated the move with haste, as if he hadn't eaten for a long time. Then again.

He put the fork down and gulped some water.

What am I going to do with that little bitch? Big mouth bitch. She was kind of cute, too, as I recall. I can put an end to that. No more cute for her.

He resumed his attack on the clam basket, finishing it. The waitress saw him and figured he was ready for the check. "Anything else, love?" she asked, putting the slip from her pad in front of him.

"Ah, no, I'm good. Thanks."

He gulped more water and reached into his jeans pocket, pulling out a wad of bills. He checked the slip and put down some cash with enough for a small tip. *The old broad's got to make a living, I guess. I know another waitress who's never going to be an old broad. Hear me, bitch?*

Chapter Thirty-Four

Back at his apartment, he took a large scrapbook from his bedroom bookshelf and brought it out to his kitchen, settled into a chair at the table and began flipping the pages. Each page contained newspaper clippings about crimes in Boston, dating back ten years. Many were about homicides involving gangland figures. There were also stories about bank robberies, extortion cases, knifings and gang fights. A prominent name in many of the stories was Tommy Shea, of Somerville. Some included the name of a police detective named Contino.

Nothing in that scrapbook caught his fancy. He needed something special for the waitress with the big mouth, so he went back into his bedroom, put the book back in its place and grabbed another scrapbook off the shelf.

Maybe this baby will have some good ideas for me. Come on, baby, cough up some good stuff for me.

He laid it on the kitchen table and stood with one knee propped on the chair. He flipped the pages slowly, eliminating candidate stories. These clippings dealt with more homicides and assaults, but not many were related to Boston gangland activities. They covered civilian crimes, for the most part, such as stabbings and shootings at bars or private parties, street fights and brawls, rapes, murders and the bizarre.

Aha, now there we go. Let's take a close look at this one. I remember that case. Why didn't I think of that right away? Yeah, baby.

He swung his leg over the chair and sat down, never taking his eyes off the page that had caught his attention.

". . . the killer may have performed an ancient burial rite over Miss England's body after they found iodine oxide, a reddish-brown powder, on the walls, ceiling, and floor of the apartment and on her body . . . early tribes in Persia sprinkled a similar powder, red ochre, over the bodies of their dead in order to purify the bodies and to drive off evil spirits."

The story described the brutal slaying in 1967 of a college graduate student in Boston, twenty-three year-old Barbara England, a doctoral candidate in archaeology. After being bludgeoned to death with a heavy, sharp-edged object, she was covered with a carpet and a reddish powder was sprinkled over her. The killer stayed around to perform a burial ritual on her remains. Because foreign born students were among her friends and school mates, the FBI got involved in the investigation. A local, MDC Police Detective, Jack Contino, worked with the Bureau. The killer was never found, however.

Yes. Yes. Yes. This is perfect, for me. Contino was even involved in this one. Need a blanket or a small rug, something Arab looking. A magic carpet, baby. I got to visit J-Mart for that. They should have something cheap that fits the bill. Maybe a hatchet, too. Hope there's a special. Thank you, J-Mart shoppers. Paprika mixed with a little salt should produce a reddish brown powder. Off to the grocery store, too. Maybe I should dress like Karnac The Magnificent for this one. Whack the girlie, spread the powder, a little Arab mumbo jumbo and away we go. Figure it out, Jacko boy. Tommy's going to love it.

He went into the bedroom, put the scrapbook back in its place and danced his way along the bookshelf to a metal, locking file box. He fumbled for the keychain in his pocket, produced it eventually and unlocked the box. Reaching in, he extracted a handful of bills, counted out an amount that suited him and thrust the bills into his left front pocket. He locked the box, smiling. Jangling the keys in his hand, he sang to himself as he hoofed his way out to the Nova. "Talkin 'bout A-Hab, the A-Rab, King of the burnin' sands... da dadee da, da dadee da, da dadee da dada."

The J-Mart store was in a strip shopping center on Rte. 132 in Hyannis, across from the Cape Cod Mall. He grabbed a shopping cart in the entranceway and hummed as he pushed it up the center aisle, looking left and right.

Rugs, rugs, where do they keep rugs?

He didn't realize that he was mumbling out loud until a thin man in an orange store vest spoke to him. "Down to your right to Housewares, sir. Watch for the sign overhead."

The man smiled at the customer and pointed in that direction.

"What? Oh, ah, yeah, thanks. I got it." As he got further away from the store employee, he dropped the friendly pretense. *What's he, a freaking mind reader? Mind your own business, low life, or you'll get yours.*

He found the collection of carpets and skimmed the aisle. His search led to a multicolored throw rug, about two feet by four feet. With lots of red, brown and black colors and circular patterns on it, the carpet looked to him like something that would suffice. He dumped it into the shopping cart.

He turned and cruised his way back down the long aisle that ran the width of the store, watching the signs above for the hardware department. As he passed by Sporting Goods, he abruptly stopped his forward motion, like slamming on the brakes. He turned his cart down that aisle, locking his gaze onto camping equipment. Among the pieces of camping gear, he spotted a hatchet.

There we are.

It was a foot long and less than two pounds, with a three inch blade and a wooden handle. He liked it. It cost a little more than he expected, but he fell in love with this inanimate object.

Oh, come to Papa, little baby. You are mine. I wish your price tag was a bit lower, but you'll be worth it. You add value to my life, sweet piece of wood and steel. Let's go home.

After arming himself with paprika from a grocery store, he traveled back to his apartment and awaited the night. His mission, however, would not be accomplished tonight. He had to stake out the Sand Dune again and watch for her movements. Tonight, he would learn of her exiting routine and follow her home. Did she drive herself to and from work? Did she live alone, and where? Once he knew these things, he would be ready to attack his target.

Chapter Thirty-Five

I would have preferred to swallow another bourbon, to mix with the two I had already enjoyed while Nat slept. But the phone call from the night dispatcher shook me sober. Another brutal killing. I arrived at the murder scene just after one o'clock in the morning. It was a small, one bedroom cottage two blocks away from West Dennis Beach. Pretty empty neighborhood this time of year. If I were going to commit a murder, I couldn't ask for a much better place than this.

The on-scene officer made the identification, but the name meant nothing to him. He knew, however, that I had to be called in because of the brutal nature of the crime. Sgt. Jim Pearson had also been called in. I had given orders to call him on anything that required my presence. He had arrived a few minutes before me.

I parked beside the police cruisers out front and nodded to the officers stationed there as I hurried into the cottage. Voices from the bedroom gave me a homing signal, which I followed. Pearson was standing just inside the bedroom door, watching as the Medical Examiner and a photographer did their chores.

"What have we got, Jim? Dispatch said it was pretty bad."

"This one's bad news, Jack, in a couple of ways." Pearson is normally staid on the job, very professional and straight forward, but his voice was off kilter somehow.

I peered over his shoulder, as he stood facing me. I saw a lot of blood around the head of the victim. "Well, let's have it, Jim. Start with the name."

"Jack, it's Gail Devereaux, the waitress at the Sand Dune, the one who told you about hearing the name Tommy Shea being yelled out during the attack on George Rogers."

In an instant, my blood ran cold. My mind raced with possibilities. I looked at Jim Pearson in disbelief.

"Damn it, damn it, damn it. I told that reporter there could be trouble from her story. This kid hears the name Tommy Shea during Rogers' attack, she writes it in the paper and now the kid is dead. I hope she's happy now. I hope she hears this on her scanner and gets sick. I hope she realizes she could be next. I hope . . . damn it, I don't know what I hope."

"Take it easy, Jack." Pearson grabbed my shoulders as if he was about to shake me, but decided not to try. "I hate to tell you this, but it gets worse."

I was staring at the floor, taking deep breaths, searching for self-control. I found some of it and looked back at Jim. "How much worse?"

We moved closer to the bed where Ms. Devereaux lay. She was flat on her back, naked, hands folded together across her chest, fingers intertwined. She had a gag pulled tight into her mouth and wrapped around her head, feet tied at the ankles. Her face was clean and unmarked, but her head was surrounded in a pool of blood that extended down to her shoulders. A reddish powder was scattered in an arch around her head, like a halo. More powder covered her chest under her hands. There was a small carpet on the floor beside the bed, also with red powder and a strong smell. I looked at the M.E., who was hovering over the victim. He straightened up and looked at me. He handed me some plastic gloves, like the ones he and Pearson were already wearing.

"We found her like this, only with that carpet covering her face and body, down to her knees," he said to me as I worked my hands into the gloves. They don't make those things in my size.

I stared at the M.E. "Go on."

"She was struck multiple times on the back of the head, with a very sharp object, an axe of some kind, not too big, maybe a camping axe or hatchet. There are drops of blood on the floor from the bathroom and there's a white nightgown over there on the floor." He pointed.

Jim Pearson spoke up. "It looks like she was surprised coming out of the bathroom and struck once, knocking her down, but not out. He must have stripped her and put her on the bed."

The M.E. took another turn. "There are marks around each wrist, suggesting that her hands had been tied at one point."

I took in the scene for a moment. "So, he knocked her out with a blow from the hatchet, stripped her, put her on the bed face up and tied and gagged her. He wanted her to wake up before he killed her, so she would know what was going to happen. What a sick bastard."

"I'm afraid so, Detective," said the M.E. "He must have taunted her in some way, for who-knows-whatever reason. My skills only help us know what, not why things are done by criminals."

I walked around the foot of the bed, eyeing the nightgown, and then walked back to the doorway, looking down the hall to the bathroom. I moved back into the bedroom and looked at Pearson. "You won't have to look too hard into your files on this one, Jimbo."

"What do you mean, Jack?"

"I remember one like this before in Boston. It was a long time ago, but it was so bizarre, you just don't forget it. A young woman, a grad student, was murdered and some sort of ritual was performed over her. A reddish powder was sprinkled around and her body was covered by a carpet. This is so much like it, I can't believe it."

"You're not thinking it's the same guy," said Jim.

"No, way too long ago. And there was no tying and gagging. This is more likely a copycat. And he may be even more sick than the original. Who found the body?"

"There's a couple outside in my squad car, a guy and a girl," said Jim. "They didn't want to wait in the house, but I'll bring them in now if you're ready to talk to them."

"Bring them into the living room. It's too cold out there."

Jim walked the couple into the house and I motioned for them to sit on the sofa. They were a good looking couple; the guy, about five foot ten, with short blond hair, wearing tan Levis and a black turtleneck sweater. He had on penny loafers without socks. I thought that look had gone out years ago. Maybe this kid was slow on the fashion uptake.

The girl had on tight red jeans and a blue hooded sweatshirt, with white sneakers and no socks. I didn't care for the hoodie look. It rubbed me the wrong way nowadays.

They told me through cracking voices that they had been waiting for a call from Gail and were going to pick her up to go to a party. When Gail didn't call, they decided to come over anyway. When they found her, they ran out of the house, both screaming into the empty neighborhood. When they calmed down, the guy went back into the house to use the phone. The girl stayed outside and vomited. They were careful not to touch anything else, except the doorknob on the front door.

The couple gave us all the information they could, which included the fact that she was a native Cape Codder and her parents lived in Brewster. The killer was long gone and we needed to finish examining the scene, so I sent them home. Once again, I had a tough phone call to make.

There was no sign of the weapon, but one officer saw something useful. There was a partial footprint on the blood trail that led from the hall to the bedroom. When he first struck her on the head, she fell and deposited some blood at that spot. The killer picked her up to carry her to the bed and stepped in the blood, leaving the partial imprint of a sneaker tread. It wasn't much, but we'd take whatever clues we could get.

I let the M.E. finish at the scene and Jim agreed to write up his report before going home, so he went off to HQ.

After sniffing around the outside a little more, I was about to leave for the office, as well. I wanted to be in the PD HQ when I had to make the call to the family. The official atmosphere helped, but not by much.

I was about to get in my car when a civilian car pulled up to the scene. I saw Lynn Bradford behind the wheel. I called out to all the officers. "Do not let this reporter on the property. Keep her behind the yellow tape and the same for anyone else who shows up. I want two duty officers here all night to maintain the crime scene. Whatever you do, DO NOT TALK TO ANY REPORTERS, especially this one. Do I make myself clear? Good."

She got out of her car and ran up to mine, but I was in it before she caught up. "Jack, wait. I have a right to know what's going on. It's news, Jack, whether you like it or not."

I never acknowledged her as I pulled away. There was enough on my mind without having to deal with the Press tonight.

Once at HQ, I decided to make the phone call immediately and searched for the phone book.

"Don't bother, Jack. I'll take care of it," said Jim Pearson from his desk. "Really, go home. You're on edge, so go home and get some rest. There'll be plenty to do tomorrow and you need to be fresh. I'll handle it."

I started to object, but Jim would have none of it. He was about fifteen years younger than me and I guess his energy supply was better. I felt myself weaken, partly due to the strain and fatigue and partly from the assurance that Jim definitely could handle it. He was one hell of a cop. I gave in.

At home, I'd kick my shoes off, knock down some whiskey and let my mind take me to a calmer, more peaceful place. It wouldn't last long. I only had time for a few hours of sleep, but I'd be home in the morning with Natalie. I could recharge my batteries before facing another hellish day.

Chapter Thirty-Six

It was quiet when he got back to his apartment in Hyannis. There were two other apartments in his building and all lights were off, as best he could see. There wasn't much night life for those tenants.

He slipped the key into his door, opened the lock and entered like a polite neighbor does. The fridge was his first stop. Grabbing a beer and popping the top, he sipped it at first and then gulped a mouthful of cold brew. His breathing was heavy and quick. The rush he felt hadn't died down yet. He paced the floor and swallowed more beer.

What a night. What a freakin' night. It was a perfect job. I'm a freakin' bloody genius. The perfect fit for that mouthy little bitch. A blast from the past, it'll get those boys in blue scratching their heads. The big guy's really going to be pissed. Right out of his own case files, a chick gets iced by some Arab nut case, eh, Jack. Is he still around? Ha ha ha. You're going to be wondering about that, Jacko, yes you are.

He polished off the beer, crushed the can in his hands, dropping it on the kitchen table, and grabbed another. In a rush to drink, he slobbered some down his front.

Ah, shit. What the hell. This is a celebration, a CELEBRATION. Here's to me, the best in the business. Yes sirree, old Tommy Boy Shea's going to beg me to join his crew. With Sammy White in the klink, he's got room for a new man, somebody who can get the job done, any kind of job. Getting close to time to really show him. Time to shake up Mr. Big Cop. Who will it be? Maybe Officer Tight Pants, ooooh, that'd be good, real good. Or maybe somebody else. Got to be careful. Don't get too close, yet. Don't want to scare him too much. Got to keep him worried.

The beer kept flowing and the number of crushed cans littered the table and spilled onto the floor. He found a bag of chips, ripped it open and settled into a chair in the small living room. The one-man celebration continued until he couldn't keep his eyes open anymore. More liquid dribbled onto his chest and crumbs decorated his shirt. His head fell back against the chair and his beer can slid out of the hand that dangled by his side, splashing cheap brew onto the floor. The self-proclaimed best in the business, heir to Sammy White's position at Tommy Shea's side, slobbed his way into a night of oblivion.

Chapter Thirty-Seven

The day couldn't start any worse than this. When I entered the lobby at HQ in the morning, there was Lynn Bradford waiting for me, sitting on a wooden bench against the wall. She sprang to her feet when she spotted me and hurried over to me. I didn't break stride as I kept on target for my office.

"Keep this bi . . . woman away from me. She's not welcome around here."

There is a wooden railing, about three feet high, with a gate. It runs wall-to-wall across the outer lobby, flanking the reception desk. I passed through the gate and let it swing closed.

"Okay, Jack, you can hate me all you want, but I've still got a job to do."

Lynn Bradford stopped short of the gate when I turned back to face her.

"Oh, you've got a job to do, all right."

"Hey, I don't feel any better about this latest killing than you do. I know who it is. I talked to Gail about the attack on Rogers. I can't believe this has happened. I'm so sorry, but I can't stop doing my job. The public has a right to know what's going on."

"Maybe in a way you're right. The public should know that you talked to Gail Devereaux and printed a story letting the world know that she was the closest thing we had to a witness in Rogers' attack, that you told everyone that she heard the name Tommy Shea, the number one Mob boss in New England, and now she's dead because of it. Does the public have a right to know any more that could get an innocent person killed?"

"That's not fair, Jack. You can't blame the Press every time a witness is harmed or threatened. There's a bigger story here than just Gail's death. Something's going on and I need to find out what. We need to work together on this."

"Work together? That's rich." I was reaching my limit with Bradford. I slammed my right fist into my left hand. "I thought we were working together, until you went behind my back. That's it. We're done." I turned and hurried through the door that led to the office area I shared with Pearson. Lynn Bradford persisted, pounding at my back.

"I'm not giving up, Jack. Your Public Information Officer will have to tell me something. This is news, Jack. Do you hear me? News."

"Yes, its news, but tell me, Lynn, when does news become poison? When does informing the public put somebody in harm's way? I tried to get you to lay back on this to protect the public and I thought you agreed with me—as in we had an agreement. Your zeal to be the ace reporter got a girl killed. Can't you see that?"

I turned away and headed for my office. "Aw, what's the use?" I grumbled. Before I got there, Bradford called to me again. Her voice was different this time, as if something in her had left.

"Jack, wait. I wasn't trying to be the ace reporter, really."

"Weren't you?" I replied, turning to face her from a distance. Her arms were limp at her sides and her face was empty.

"I . . . I'm sorry, Jack. I never thought Gail would get hurt. You have to believe me."

I took a breath. "We all have to take responsibility for our actions, Lynn. Sometimes that means thinking things through before we act. Your actions . . . well, we know what happened. Go home, Lynn. Get some rest and think about it."

She stood there, alone in the lobby, her lower lip starting to quiver like a child who just got a scolding from Dad. She stood still momentarily before turning silently and leaving. Perhaps I had gotten through to her, maybe not. Either way, she wouldn't get much from the PIO.

The PIO had orders not to talk about the ritual over Gail Devereaux. Just give out the bare minimum about the case. We didn't need to have the rest come out yet, not in an ongoing investigation.

I entered my office area and poured a cup of coffee. There were times when I understood the job the Press had to do and other times, I hated them. No question about this time. Bradford had broken our deal, had interviewed Gail Devereaux and printed too much information without clearing it through me, as she had agreed to. And now, Gail was dead. The ritualistic nature of it was a diversionary tactic, I was sure. But why that particular ritual? Could it just be coincidence that it resembled a case of mine from over forty years ago? Not likely, but still, it was hard to figure.

When Jim Pearson showed up for work, I was on my second coffee. He looked fine and alert for a guy who had short sleep and tough duty the night before. If I looked like I felt, mothers would hide their children from the sight of me. He looked at me with a tight grin, skipping the morning pleasantries.

There was a legal yellow pad of paper in my center desk drawer, which I pulled out and flopped onto my desk. Scribbling some notes on it was a way of trying to pull my thoughts together, but nothing made sense to me. I looked over at Pearson in a silent call for help.

"Through all the other killings, the only link was the guy in the hooded sweatshirt. Now we have two attacks on people who worked at The Sand Dune, a much stronger connection, and the hooded guy may be linked to both, but why?" said Jim.

"And don't forget the Tommy Shea thing," I added. "What's he got to do with this? Anything? I don't like the fact that he may have extended his drug business to the Cape. But I can't see a connection."

"But that doesn't mean it's not there," said Jim. "We know he's moved his drug business onto the Cape and suddenly there are these killings. Then, the attempt on Rogers and Shea's name is yelled out loud and the waitress who tells that to the press gets killed. Her killer has to be the guy who attacked Rogers. Her name wasn't mentioned in the newspaper, so the guy must have known who she was, because he saw her the night he attacked Rogers. It's screwy, Jack, but somehow these things are related."

"Even the earlier killings, Robert Schroeder and Blake Hairston? Grant Bartlett, maybe, but those first two just don't seem to belong in the picture. Why did Hoodie kill them?"

"I don't know, Jack, but we're going to find out. I've got to hit the head, then we'll get to work."

As Pearson walked away, I reached into my bottom desk drawer and pulled out a bottle of Beam. A shot in my coffee, maybe two, would help me get started.

I sat down and scribbled some thoughts on the pad. Schroeder killing . . . looked like a Mob-type execution . . . Hairston . . . murdered and dismembered . . . Bartlett . . . businessman, sports venue owner . . . Rogers . . . witness in my case against Sidney Fish.

Maybe the bourbon was helping, because I felt that a pattern was emerging. There were murders that shared a common point with some old cases of mine. Rogers was directly involved in a recent case of mine. I needed to think this through some more. I wasn't ready to share it with Pearson, but I sensed I was on the right track.

Chapter Thirty-Eight

Some mornings, Tommy Shea liked to go to a café on the Tufts campus, near his hometown of Somerville. It was an old wooden building with a blue exterior, located on College Avenue near the M&S Bank. The café was in the lower level beneath the post office. Students used it for morning coffee, snacks and lunch. Some townspeople frequented the place, too, like Shea, who lived one town over and knew a good thing when he saw it. The coeds provided ample eye candy for him. Sometimes, he could entice a few very bright but not-so-smart young men into a brief morning card game with him. A fool and his money, as they say.

He sat at a table near a wall, his back to it, so he could see all who came and went. The wooden chairs, painted blue like the interior, had a padded seat under a yellow vinyl cover. Bobby Sullivan was sitting across from Shea reading a newspaper. Shea's eyes moved from side to side, taking in all the movement of student patrons, a blank expression on his face masking his pleasure.

"Hey Tommy, would you look at this," said Bobby. He put the newspaper flat on the table and lowered his head, as if he was about to sniff the ink. "A chick was killed on the Cape the other night and she worked at a bar called the Sand Dune. That's the same place where a guy was attacked and somebody called out your name."

"What? Let me hear it." Shea redirected his eyes toward Bobby.

"That's about all it says. She was killed at her house, beat with a club or something, at night. It says she was a waitress at the Sand Dune. Remember that attack on the bartender, where somebody called out your name? The waitress described somebody in jeans and a dark hooded sweatshirt, like that guy who came into Club 77 and bought you a drink and hit the street."

Shea stared at Bobby. "Yeah, that guy."

"Tommy, this is bad. This guy is popping people and leaving a trail with your name. Maybe we should go after him." Bobby slapped his fingers backhanded at the newspaper, as if he were hitting somebody.

"That son-of-a-bitch," said Tommy. "What the hell does he think he's doing?" Shea spread his hands, palms down, on the table. "At first, I thought he might be a cop, but cops don't go around wasting people. He's got to be a freelancer. But what's he up to, getting my name mixed up in his business?" His voice grew loud enough for others to look away from their own conversations and glance at him.

Bobby noticed the stares and dropped the volume, looking left and right. "Come on, Tommy, let's go get him. You know where he lives. Let's take care of this guy before he does some more damage."

Shea made a fist and slammed it into his other hand. He held it there, turning the fist. A few seconds passed before he spoke.

"No, not yet." He moved his head halfway across the table at Bobby. "I want to know more about this guy before I make a move. Besides, if the cops think I'm linked to him and I go waste him, they'll be right. I know Contino. He'll expect me to make a move. Maybe this story is bait. Well, I won't take it. I'm not biting. No, we're not moving on that freelancer just yet. The Feds are nosing around D'Agostino's place on the Cape, so Contino can't be far away. He works with the Feds a lot. Maybe it's Contino we should be watching. You know, the hunter becomes the hunted, so to speak. I'll go to the Cape, but just to get more information. I've got to figure this guy out."

Bobby smiled. He didn't quite understand Shea's logic, but he smiled just the same. If Shea thought it was good, it must be.

"Let's get out of here," said Tommy. "I want to think some more about how to handle this. I can't think here. Too many distractions."

As they reached the exit, Shea turned around to get another glance at the young patrons. He noticed a tall, shapely girl, about five-foot ten, with long black hair down almost to her waist, standing next to a table, talking to friends. She had on a white turtleneck sweater and a brown miniskirt that fit snug against her body.

"I like this place a lot," said Shea. "When I'm here, I see a bright future." The girl overheard him and looked his way. Her eyes caught Tommy's for a second and her lips broke into a slight grin. Tommy always had an eye opened toward the future.

Chapter Thirty-Nine

Natalie wasn't home when I got to the house after work. Sometimes she has to put in a long day and I figured that was the case now, so I poured myself a bourbon rocks and stood at the kitchen breakfast counter, sipping my drink as if I were at a friendly bar. I guess I was.

I glanced toward the living room and the big, inviting easy chair, but decided against dropping into it. I might have trouble staying awake and I didn't want Nat to come home and find me crashed there. *Stay on your feet, Jack, but lose the jacket.*

After some healthy sips of bourbon, I went to the fridge for more ice. That's when I noticed the note taped to the freezer door. How'd I miss that before? It said Nat was off to the grocery store to get some steaks. Leo had called just as she got home and said he was on his way and would spend the night. I must have just left the office, so he missed me there and called the house.

I figured Leo must have some news for me to justify a road trip. I hoped it was something good. I hadn't seen my old friend for a while, so I was happy to have a chance to drink up with the guy.

I was halfway through my drink when Nat's car pulled into the driveway. I opened the door for her and took the bundle from her arms, gave her a smooch and carried the bag over to the counter. She hung up her coat on the rack next to the door and eased her way toward me. She fit nicely into my gentle bear hug, her feet leaving the ground. Her body felt great against me and I closed my eyes, hoping this time could stretch on to infinity.

"You know, big guy, I hope the day never comes when you can't do this to me anymore. But, that said, I'll have a tough time cooking dinner while still airborne. Time for a two-point landing, lover." She kissed my cheek and then patted my shoulder three times. I opened my eyes as we both came back to earth.

"I got a couple of thick rib eyes for you two carnivores. Be sure to leave me some scraps. Say Jack, it'll be at least an hour before Leo gets here, so go slow on the Beam, okay? I know you'll have a few more once he's here. I'll get the dinner started. Why don't you make yourself useful and fix up the guest room? We don't want Leo to think we run a shabby joint, now do we?"

"I'm on it, Boss." Nat always knew how to keep me focused.

Leo arrived just before seven o'clock. Nat had already made a salad, and potatoes were baking in the oven, so she started frying some onion and mushrooms before getting to the steaks.

I had the front door opened for him as he approached the house, carrying a small overnight case in one hand and a garment bag slung over his shoulder. He walked straight past me. "Thank you, boy. You'll get a good tip when I check out."

"The way you tip, I better not quit my day job," I said.

He dropped the garment bag on a living room chair, placed the overnight bag next to it on the floor and went into his greeting mode. Leo's smile could light up a room. "Glad ta see ya," he said, in a mock Phil Silvers style. We shook hands and enjoyed a man hug, like old buddies will do.

"Oooh, the smell of fried onions always gets my attention," he said. "I guess I know where Nat is." He turned and made a bee line for the kitchen, with me following. Nat was at the stove, stirring the veggies in a skillet.

"Could I interest you in a drink, Mr. Barbado?" I asked.

"Hold on there, good sir. First things first. Right now, I have to go put a move on your wife."

Nat turned toward Leo, feigning surprise. "Oh, my dear Mr. Barbado, I do declare."

They embraced, and Nat planted a kiss on Leo's cheek. He pulled his head back, smiling. "Hey, I just happen to have another one of those over here," he said, turning to the other side. Nat obliged and kissed him again.

"Unhand the woman, friend. I have a claim on her. Besides, whiskey awaits."

Leo turned to me, still holding Nat in his arms. "So you do, sir." He turned back to Natalie. "Sorry, my dear, but it seems you're spoken for and there's a glass over there with my name on it. I'll let you go about your task whilst the man over there fills it up."

I poured two bourbon on the rocks, and motioned Leo into the dining room, where the table was already set for three. I sat at one end and Leo took up his place to my right. "Here's to old friends and good times," I said, raising my glass.

"Here, here," said Leo. We touched our glasses and sipped our drinks, enjoying the moment, or was it a second?

"I'm glad you're here, Leo. The situation is getting bad. You know about Gail Devereaux?" He nodded and sipped bourbon again. "I was hoping your trip tonight meant you'd got something new about Shea."

"I wish I could say yes to that. Actually, I'm here because I don't have anything and it's getting annoying. Watching Shea for telltale moves has been like watching paint dry. I know Agent Nelson figured something would happen after Billy D'Agostino got aced, but nothing, zippo. Shea's just going about his usual business, hanging out with his buddies and hitting Club 77 at night. I needed a change of scene, Jack. Actually, I figured maybe I could sit down with you and go over this thing from the top down. There's got to be a piece that we're missing."

"I read you on that, Leo. Pearson and I have talked about that, too. We can't find any connection between our guy in the hooded sweatshirt and Tommy Shea. And we can't figure Shea's in on any of the other killings that Mr. Hoodie has done. So, what's the missing piece?"

Leo was about to answer when Nat emerged carrying a platter with the steaks. I took the cue and rose out of my chair, headed into the kitchen and scooped up the salad bowl and the bottles of dressing that were next to it. As I reentered the dining room, Nat passed me going back for the veggies. Once all the food was on the table, I offered to freshen up Leo's drink, which he accepted. Nat had poured herself a glass of red wine. We settled in at the table, as we had done so many times over the years, and enjoyed a great meal and great friendship.

After dinner, Leo and I cleaned up the kitchen and did the dishes, while Nat drank some coffee in the living room. We talked more about the cases and how they resembled some of our old ones.

"I've got some more thoughts on our friend Mr. Shea," said Leo. Before he could get any further with his ideas, Nat came into the kitchen. "Grab your drinks and follow me, boys. I've got some ground rules to cover." She marched us to the living room.

"Okay, you two, here's the deal," she said. "Put your butts down and get comfortable. You're going to have all day tomorrow to talk shop, so tonight, we're all going to sit and enjoy each other's company. Casablanca is on TV tonight and it's been ages since I've seen it. You always liked that movie, too, Jack, so you guys will have to hold your cops and robbers stuff for later. Got it?"

Leo and I looked at each other, wondering which of us would speak. He gave me that look that says, "Not me, partner."

I took the lead and nodded to Natalie. "That sounds like a fair deal, hon."

Leo shrugged in agreement and took a drink. "This sounds like the beginning of a beautiful friendship."

I sat next to Natalie on the sofa and Leo eased his way into the big recliner. We settled in for an easy night. The hard stuff was yet to come.

Chapter Forty

Leo followed me into headquarters the next morning and we met with Jim Pearson and Karen Orlando to go over the case. We had to bust through this dilemma before there was another murder. I felt like time was rushing past me and running out on the next victim.

The small conference room became our meeting place, after we grabbed our coffees. I took the notepad from my desk and Pearson carried a cardboard file box, loaded with his press clippings and other notes. Leo had helped out on a recent case, so everybody knew him. No need for introductions.

Leo and I sat on one side of the conference table, Orlando and Pearson sat across from us. I took the lead. "The only thing that makes sense in this case is that Tommy Shea is involved in it, somehow. Mr. Hoodie called out his name for a reason when attacking George Rogers. It doesn't mean that Shea is personally involved in any of the killings. But somehow, he's got to be connected to our killer. Leo, along with the FBI, has been watching Shea since the Billy D'Agostino hit up in Boston. Shea's name is on the deed of the house Billy D. was using to run drugs in Dennis. So, now we know Shea has an operation on the Cape. I believe that our best bet for finding our sweatshirt guy is through Shea."

Pearson and Orlando nodded. "So, what do we do, put a shadow on him?" asked Jim.

"Leo and the FBI have already been doing that, but so far, he hasn't made a move," I said. "Leo, you want to bring them up to speed?"

Leo explained about the surveillance.

"It's been pretty dull, so far. Shea's playing it cool, but here's something I saved for today, Jack."

I lowered my head for a moment. "Leo, I knew you didn't show up just to drink my booze. Let's hear it."

Leo sat up straight, as if getting ready to make a speech. He was looking quite pleased with himself.

"I have a theory," he said. "What I've seen of Shea via a few stakeout sessions is that he goes out wearing a dark overcoat, a knitted hat and dark glasses. He turns his collar up and there isn't much of his face showing. He never took that much trouble before to cover up his identity. Agent Nelson and his boys aren't sure about it. Me, I figure he's setting things up to use an imposter to draw us away while he makes his move, whatever that might be. I figure he's headed for the Cape. If he's got a new associate down here, he's got to make contact with him soon. So why stay in Somerville? I figured I'd be, what do they say now, proactive. He's going to show his face here, so why not get ahead of him?"

The group was silent for a few seconds before Orlando spoke. "Mr. Barbado, that makes sense, but how can we know when he'll come here or where he'll show up?"

Leo looked at me. "Jack, care to answer that one?"

When you've worked with a guy for decades, you start to know how each other thinks. As soon as Leo had finished his comments, I knew where he was going, but he turned it over to me so I'd get the kudos from my people. It was like a marriage. I tapped my fingers on the table and nodded to Leo before facing the others. "If I were a betting man, I'd figure Shea will want to know more about what happened at the Sand Dune. He won't go there, but he knows who's already been looking into it."

"But that means us," said Karen. "He's not going to show his face at police HQ."

"No, he's not," I said. "But there is somebody else. Lynn Bradford's the reporter who wrote the stories in the Boston paper. Shea's smart enough to track her down. He probably already knows that she works at the Cape Cod *Times*. There's a good chance that Shea will pay her a visit, just to talk, I hope. Karen, I want you to talk to her. Let her know about this and tell her to call us immediately if she hears from Shea."

"Will do, Jack," said Karen. "What about George Rogers? Do you think he'll try to contact George?"

"No, there's still a police guard posted with Rogers, so Shea won't make that mistake," I said. "Leo, now it's my turn."

Leo sat back in his chair and smiled, as if he knew this was coming. "I've been waiting for this, partner. After all, I didn't come all the way down here just to drink your booze."

I worked my way out of my chair and strode over to the wall covered by a long white board. Chalkboards were out nowadays and good riddance. I hated getting that chalk dust all over my suit. You couldn't help it. That stuff was like spring pollen. I grabbed a red dry-erase marker and pulled off the top cover.

I wrote the first victim's name on the board . . . Robert Schroeder. Beside it, I wrote the words Mob Hit and underlined it. "Our killer made this look like a Mob hit, done professional style, up close and personal, like the victim knew his killer and let him in the house. That was our stock 'n trade, Leo, a typical case for many years."

Leo nodded and the others were still.

"The second is a woman who he strangles and dismembers. We had one like that, Leo, you even reminded me of that when I told you about it. These murders are nothing alike, except that a guy in a hooded sweatshirt was spotted at the scene and the cases are similar to ones I've had before."

Leo scratched his chin.

"Then a rich guy who owns part of a sports complex gets it. His financing is from the Mob. He gets killed and dumped in the river. That's like the Jai Alai fronton owner in Rhode Island in 1968. He was owner of the place until certain characters from Somerville forced their way into the business. The guy was a reluctant partner, so reluctant that he wound up in the Charles River. Gambling is watched by the FBI, so I got called in to help with the Somerville connection."

Leo moved forward in his chair and rested his elbows on the table.

"Each of these murders on the Cape has a similarity to cases I've worked on in my career," I said.

Leo tapped the table with a fingertip. "And George Rogers was our witness against Sidney Fish in the case with the neo-Nazi creeps," he said. "That's not a similarity, Jack. It's a real case of yours, not long ago. He's getting closer."

"Yes, real close," I said. "And he's going to get closer, because I believe I'm his ultimate target. He's eventually coming for me."

A loud silence came over the room. Leo broke it.

"Jack, I hate to state the obvious, but there are several layers between Rogers and you. There could be one or more preliminaries before he tries you. Look at that waitress who he killed."

"I know, Leo. But Gail Devereaux wasn't a target. She was someone who got in the way because of Lynn Bradford's article exposing her. The guy panicked and thought he'd better shut her up."

Karen Orlando looked hard at Leo. "So you think he could come after someone else who's close to Jack, like a family member or . . . a colleague."

Leo lowered his voice as he stared back at Orlando. "Yes. That's right." Orlando swallowed hard.

I turned back to the white board and added the names George Rogers and Gail Devereaux, side-by-side. Below those names I wrote Orlando, Pearson, Barbado and Natalie, all on one line.

Pearson spoke up. "You really think he'd try to get your wife, Jack?" Typical of a good cop, Pearson's first thought was about somebody else. He skipped right over his own name.

"I do, Jim. That's why I'm sending her off Cape to her sister in Medford, only she doesn't know it yet. And that's why everybody in this room and on the Dennis PD travels in pairs now. Karen, when you go to see Lynn Bradford, Jim goes with you."

"Got it, Chief," she said.

Leo looked around the room, as if he was examining all the faces. "Jack, we seem to have gotten away from the Tommy Shea thing. I'm with you, so far, on the path this nut case is going to follow. But we still haven't established the link to Shea. The thing that comes to mind to me is that Shea's pal, Sammy White, put a contract out on you during the neo-Nazi case. Do you think this is a follow-up, that the hoodie guy is a contractor for Shea?"

"No, I don't," I said. "Mob guys want their hits to be quick and clean, no fuss and very little muss. Mr. Hoodie is too slow and methodical. He's not a serial killer. The Gail Devereaux murder proves that. Her killing came with a reason. In fact, they all did. They were very calculated. He was following a pattern that was practically invisible. There was a common thread, but we couldn't see it, until now. I'm that thread."

"But how does that connect to Tommy Shea?" asked Orlando.

"Leo," I said, "you want the floor?"

"Got my dancing shoes on just in case you asked, Jack. Each of the cases that Jack mentioned from his, our, past history, involved Tommy Shea as a suspect, involved in some way. With that woman being dismembered, for example. We believe that he helped a crony of his kill the other guy's ex-girlfriend. We got the word from a snitch who led us to where her body parts were found, including her head. Dental records gave us the ID, but we had no proof of who did it. It would be the snitch's word against the other two. Shea and his buddy skated."

"So, what do you see as the connection here?" said Pearson.

Leo looked at me before continuing. "I believe what Jack is driving at is that we have a wannabe on our hands."

Orlando looked perplexed. "A what?"

"A wannabe," I said, still standing at the board. Orlando was learning the job well, but she had a long way to go. "Mr. Hoodie is trying to impress Shea, for whatever reason. Maybe he thinks Shea will hire him. He couldn't contain his excitement when he attacked Rogers and called out Shea's name during the attack. Shea and I are the common threads in each of these recent murders and the attempt on George Rogers. He must follow Shea in the newspapers and TV, sort of the twisted opposite of Pearson and his files. That's how he knows who I am and what I mean to Shea. We're archenemies. The guy thinks it will be the ultimate prize for him to bring to Shea if he kills me. But it's not going to happen."

"So, what's the plan, Jack, to stop Mr. Hoodie?" said Jim.

"We watch each other's backs, real close. I'm going to send Nat away and a uniformed officer is going to accompany her. Her car is going to stay at the house. Leo's car can stay here at headquarters and he'll ride with me. Orlando, I'm going to get another female officer to stay at your place for a few days. Jim, I want another officer staying at your house for a while, too. You can travel to work together. I still believe I'm the next and final target, but let's play it safe."

"That's why I always pack a bag when I visit Jack," said Leo. "I never know how long he's going to need my expertise." His voice had the usual wisecrack edge to it.

"You really think he's coming soon, Jack?" said Jim.

"Yes, I do. The story exposing Gail Devereaux threw him off. He knows we're going into high alert after that. He doesn't have as much freedom to set things up now. He's got to make his move. My guess is just a couple of days."

Chapter Forty-One

Nat didn't take the news very well.

"What do you mean I have to visit my sister? How bad is this thing getting, Jack?"

It was mid-morning and we were at her workplace. Leo waited in my car. We were standing in a vacant examining room, door closed. I had explained to the doc that I needed to talk to Natalie and pull her out of work for a few days.

"We've got things under control, hon, really," I said, wishing I were a better actor. "That's why Leo is here."

"Be straight with me, mister. You're sending me away because you think this bad guy might actually come right to our home. You think he might attack us right there. You think that there could be gunfire in our own house."

I rubbed my hands together trying to think of something reassuring to say, something positive. I could say the guy sometimes uses a knife. That wouldn't work.

"Nat, honey, this is the best way, really. An officer is going to take you there."

"I've always been at your side, Jack Contino. I've never left you before and I don't want to start now."

Geeze, she could be stubborn.

"Leo will drive your car home and you can ride with me. The officer will meet us at the house. Now come on, hon, let's go, please."

Tears began to show in Nat's eyes. She spoke with a crack in her voice. "We're a team, Jack Contino. We've always been a team, you and me. I took care of the kids when work took you away. I sat at your bedside around the clock when you took that bullet in the gut. I know what kind of work you do and it never bothered me until that one. We agreed to move to Dennis after we talked it over, together. I want to stay, Jack."

"No dice, Nat. That won't work."

"Won't work?" she said. "I'll tell you what won't work. I don't want to be in Medford and get the phone call. You know the call I mean, Jack. I couldn't stand that."

"I won't let that happen, Nat. I promise. I'm also not going to let that nut case get to you. He's not going to get the chance to . . ."

She cut me off. "To what, Jack? To do what?" We both took deep breaths. "You're not just worried that there could be a shootout at our house. You're worried that he will come after me, specifically, aren't you? You think I could be his target. Oh, my God."

I didn't have to answer her. She knew she was right. It took a moment before I could speak.

"I . . . I can't be with you every second. I have to find this guy. I have to stop him. I have to know you're safe if I'm going to do my job. Please, Nat, don't fight me on this. This is what you have to do as my teammate now, this time."

The tears stopped and Nat's face went cold. She straightened her back in a rigid stance. She didn't speak. She just nodded slightly and moved toward the door. I began to follow her, when she stopped and turned. She threw her arms around my neck. I took her and gently lifted her in a hug.

"Jack, I love you so much. I don't want to lose you. I don't even want to come close to that again."

"I know, hon. I love you, too. We're going to get through this. We always get through the bad stuff. We're a great team."

I held her for a moment longer. I thought of all the years we'd spent together. They all flashed by in a second. I knew that even the greatest of teams eventually came to an end.

Chapter Forty-Two

Jim Pearson drove the patrol car to the Cape Cod *Times* building with Karen Orlando. "Jim," she said as they drove through the back roads from Dennis to Hyannis, "Do you think Jack is right about him being the final target for this killer? It's really scary."

"Someday, when you have a family, then you'll really understand how scary it is. It shakes you to the bone. It's not just Jack he might target. Put yourself in Jack's shoes. He's got to worry about himself, but he's also got to worry about his wife and colleagues. There's a line from an old movie, High Noon, I think. A woman is talking to a guy who is about to run out on Gary Cooper, who is in deep trouble. She says, 'a man IS responsibility.' That's Jack. He takes responsibility and always lives up to it. He's been doing it his whole career. I've got a lot of news clippings about cases he was involved with in Boston. Heck, I knew a lot about him before I ever met him. He takes responsibility and there's a lot of pressure on a guy who does that."

Orlando looked down for a second before speaking. "I'm worried about him, Jim. I know he keeps a bottle of whiskey in his drawer."

"Hell, Karen, we all know it. He's not hiding it. Even the Chief knows. But he lets it slide because we all know about Jack. He took a bad gut shot a few years ago and he's had other close calls. He's seen a lot of real bad stuff over the years. But he's one of the most decorated cops in Boston history and he never lets a fellow officer down."

"Do you think he can handle this, you know, because his wife might be in danger?"

"He'll handle it because we're all here to help him," said Pearson.

"Jim, did he ever offer you a drink in the office?"

"Sure, a couple of times."

"Did you take it?"

Pearson glanced at Orlando and turned back to the road. "Someday, Karen, I'll bet he offers you a blast from that bottle, when he figures you've earned it."

Karen broke into a tight grin and looked straight ahead.

They arrived at the *Times* building, checked in and went to Lynn Bradford's office. She was sitting at her desk when they arrived. Orlando knocked on the open door.

Bradford looked up at the uniformed officers. "Hello. To what do I owe this visit?" She was trying to be cool, but couldn't entirely hide some concern at the sight of the police. She glanced over Orlando's shoulder, as if searching for Jack Contino. "Won't you come in and have a seat?"

There was a small sofa off to the side against the wall. Pearson sat there while Orlando eased into a chair beside the desk. It was her lead.

"Mrs. Bradford, there's been a development in the George Rogers and Gail Devereaux cases and we want you to know about it."

"No kidding," she said. "Well, that's a switch. I didn't think your boss would ever cooperate with me again. You actually have information for me that I could use?"

"Not exactly," said Orlando. "You're familiar with the name Tommy Shea, I believe."

"Yes, of course. That's the name the attacker called out when stabbing George Rogers and, what's more, I know very well who he is, famous Boston Mob guy, head of the Winter Hill gang from Somerville. What about him?"

"We have very good reason to believe he's going to try to approach you about your story."

Bradford sat up straight in her chair. "Approach me. Just what do you mean, exactly?"

"We believe he's going to try to find out everything he can about the events at the Sand Dune. We don't think he's actually involved, but somebody has brought his name into the picture and, most likely, he's not happy about that."

Bradford began to fidget with her hands and tapped her pen against her desk repeatedly, like a drummer. "Do you think I'm in any kind of danger from Mr. Shea?"

Orlando looked over at Pearson before answering. "It's hard to predict what Shea will do in any scenario. He is a bit of a hair trigger. But we think he just wants to talk to you. There'd be no advantage to attacking you. He wants to know what you know, that's all."

Lynn Bradford pushed back in her chair and breathed. "Well, what if he does approach me, as you say? What should I do?"

"Whether or not you talk to him is up to you, but I do suggest that you be careful not to anger him. Whatever the case, we want you to call us right away. We need to know when he's here on the Cape. He's been under surveillance in Boston, but we believe he'll shake that easily enough if he's coming here, and we believe he is."

Orlando got up from her chair, signaling that the visit was over. Pearson followed her lead.

"Very well, Officer, I understand. If he shows up, I'll call you right away." She stood up and offered a shaky hand to Orlando. "Thank you for the warning."

"Think of it more as a heads up, Mrs. Bradford. We don't need a 9-1-1 call. He's not a suspect, after all. We just want to be able to keep an eye on him. You understand."

"Yes, of course. Thank you again."

***

Getting out of Boston was always a pain on the Southeast Expressway, but Tommy Shea managed it while keeping his temper. He got clear of the heavy traffic as he moved past Braintree, beyond Marshfield and Plymouth. He didn't notice the nice weather or the scenery as he drove over the bridge onto Cape Cod. He was focused on the creep who called out his name while knifing a bartender. He wanted to get this guy really badly, but he had to stay cool. He wanted to know more, even though his pulse was racing.

He took the Hyannis exit off Rte. 6 and faced his dilemma. He was considering finding the reporter who wrote the story about the guy, but he was losing his patience. He had found the guy's place before and saw him at his car. Shea couldn't resist the urge to check him out again to see if he'd make a move. Watching his movements might be the best way to learn about him.

Chapter Forty-Three

It was nearing six o'clock, so Officer Orlando was getting ready to end her shift. I wanted her to wait for the second shift female officer who was assigned to stay with her overnight, but Karen griped about waiting around. I still wanted everyone on maximum alert for Mr. Hoodie, but the day had been uneventful and Karen could be persuasive when she poured on the charm.

"Really, Jack," she said, about to make her case for leaving early and alone. "Officer Heard will be here soon, but I don't see any point in my hanging around. I'd like the opportunity to tidy up my place a bit. I wasn't expecting company when I left this morning, so, please, let me head out now so I can do my thing. Jack, I'm sure Natalie would understand."

Funny how women can always find an ally when they decide to gang up on you. I knew Orlando was a tough gal, but I didn't like the idea of her not waiting for her partner.

"I've got a better idea," I said. "How about Pearson keeps you company? What the heck, he's been with you all day. He rides with you and waits for us at your place. You good with that, Jim?"

"Sure enough. And, don't worry, Karen, I won't look at anything that's . . . untidy at your place." Jim was always very accommodating.

"Fair enough, Jack," said Orlando. "But I'm sure I'd be okay by myself."

"Nothing doing. Jim, escort the young officer home. See you shortly."

They left without further discussion.

Leo had poured himself a cup of coffee and called to me from the coffee counter as I sat at my desk. "Who makes the coffee around here, Jack, Officer Orlando?"

"Hey, don't be so sexist, Leo. As a matter of fact, Pearson usually has the duty. I think he likes doing it."

"Or maybe he doesn't trust anybody else." Leo took a sip and smiled at me.

About ten minutes later, Officer Heard sprang into the office, all spit and polish and ready for duty. She was a rookie.

"Officer Heard reporting, sir. I'm ready for my assignment."

"I can see that. Good."

She was tall, about five-foot, eight inches, I'd say, with a lean build. Unlike Officer Orlando, her uniform hung on her loosely and her light brown hair was short, giving her a sort of Prince Valiant look.

"Say, how long have you been on the force now, Officer?"

"Eight months, sir."

"You been going to the range?"

"Yes, sir."

"How you been doing there?"

"Just fine, sir. I can assure you that I can hit what I'm aiming at, sir."

I stared at her without speaking. The expression on her face changed from supreme confidence to puzzlement to concern.

"Sir, whatever happens tonight, I'll be ready." Her voice cracked just a wee bit.

I liked her. "How old are you, Officer Heard?"

"Twenty-one, sir. My birthday's coming up next month."

"There going to be a party?"

"Well, I don't know, sir. I mean, maybe my family will do that, but I can't say. Or maybe my boyfriend will, but, well, I just don't know."

"You should have a party. Maybe I'll throw one for you."

"That would be nice of you, sir. Thank you for thinking of me."

I caught a glimpse of Leo out of the corner of my eye. He was enjoying my banter with Officer Heard. So was I.

"Officer, would you ask Mr. Barbado over there if he's finished with his coffee? We have to get going."

"Yes, sir. Ah, Mr. Barbado, sir, are you . . ."

Leo cut her off as he took one last gulp and dropped the plastic cup into the trash can. "Yes I am, Officer. Time to rock 'n roll."

Leo and I wore a weapon in a shoulder harness and we checked them for readiness, then slipped into our jackets and made our way to my car. "Officer Heard, you're up front," I said. Leo climbed into the back without a shrug or comment.

"Yes, sir," said Heard.

The *sir* stuff was getting old, but I figured the rookie felt comfortable with it, so I let it ride.

We rode west from the station house to Old Bass River Road and took a right and then a hard left onto a road lined with forest. We emerged onto a strip where some new houses were being built and then the road swung to the right and there was more forest on both sides. We were about a half mile from Orlando's house. We were almost out of the forested area, before Orlando's neighborhood, when I noticed a gray car stopped on the shoulder ahead of us. I looked it over as we drove by and I hit the brakes. I looked all around before putting my car into reverse.

"What gives, Jack?" said Leo.

I placed my right arm across the back of my seat as I drove backwards, craning my neck to see out the rear window. I pulled up to within a car's length of the small, gray auto. It was an old Chevy Nova.

"This could be his car," I said. "Everybody hold tight. Look around, first."

We surveyed the area from inside our car.

"It looks empty, Jack," said Leo. "Let's take a closer look."

"Officer Heard, stand in front of my car. Leo, take the passenger side. I'll take the driver side. Go easy."

We pulled out our weapons, exited the car and slowly approached the gray Nova. It looked empty, but Hoodie could be stretched out on the floor waiting for us with a gun drawn, so we moved with extreme care. I approached the driver's door but stood along the fender, peering through the front windshield. Leo mimicked my movements on the passenger side. Holding my weapon in my right hand and pointing it skyward, I put my left hand on the door handle and yanked it open. There was nobody home. Leo checked the back seat and came to the same conclusion.

It was a beat up old car, with torn upholstery and a dusty dashboard, but there was nothing else; no cans or bottles on the floor, no newspapers or magazines, no rags or articles of clothing. There was nothing that could be construed as possible evidence.

"Officer, get on the radio. Get a cruiser out here and have them stay with this vehicle." Officer Heard obeyed my order as Leo and I took a last look around, then got back in my car. "We better hurry to Orlando's place." I shot a look at Leo. His face went cold.

I floored the gas pedal, the tires making a screeching sound as we pulled back onto the road. I had a decision to make. Lights flashing and siren on. If Hoodie was there, I wanted to scare him off, rather than endanger my officers. On the other hand, he might decide to try for a quick kill before fleeing. Police work is a constant game of dice.

The road straightened out ahead and we were at Karen Orlando's place in seconds. The neighborhood was modestly developed, with houses beside hers and across the street. The yards were bordered by tall shrubs and trees. There was a car in the driveway across from Orlando's and another on the shoulder a few hundred feet up from us. I paid no attention to it, as I pulled up perpendicular to the driveway on my left, blocking Orlando's car. I killed the siren.

"Heard, get on the radio and get some backup NOW. Then watch the front from behind the vehicle. Leo, take the back of the house, I'll take the front."

Nobody answered. They just did as ordered.

I crouched down and ran up to the front door. I knew it was bad because nobody came out to see why we had lights and sirens when we arrived. Then, a gunshot. I looked back at Officer Heard, holding my hand up to keep her back. With a rush of adrenaline, I kicked the front door open, but stayed outside, anticipating shots. Nothing.

I heard a moaning sound and got on the floor to look inside. Jim Pearson was lying face down to my right on the entry room floor. He had handcuffs on his ankles and his hands were cuffed behind his back. His mouth was covered with duct tape and there was a small amount of blood trickling down the back of his head. He wasn't shot, more like a pistol whip wound. He was barely conscious.

There was no time to wait for the backup. Pearson was hurt and I couldn't know what Leo or Orlando's status was. I could only assume it was real bad. I crawled forward toward Jim. "Easy, Jimbo," I said as I got next to him. "There's more help coming." I thought about switching my gun into my left hand so that I could get my keys and uncuff Pearson. I didn't have time.

"Come out, come out, WHEREVER I AM."

I heard the crazed voice and looked up to see two people. I wanted to swing my gun around to give him the greeting he deserved, but I couldn't. I rose up on one knee, but that's all I could do. There were two people moving out of the kitchen and into the entry room. It was Mr. Hoodie all right, wearing his usual get up; jeans, sneakers and a dark hooded sweatshirt, the hood pulled tight around his head. He had Karen Orlando pinned against his front, his left arm around her waist with a knife pointed at her gut. She was stripped to the waist. There was a trickle of blood where the knife was piercing her skin. His right hand held a pistol, pointed at me.

"Good afternoon, big fella. You must be Detective Contino. It's such a pleasure to finally meet you. You know, I've followed your career for a long time. Well, that is, I've researched it a lot, going back. It's nice how the library has those microfiche readers with old newspapers on them. You can look up things that go back decades and even print out the stuff. Isn't that amazing?"

I never felt such rage in my life. I've faced down gunmen before, but never while an officer was being held and tortured like Karen. And what about Leo?

"Shoot him, Jack. Just shoot," said Orlando.

"No, no, no, Detective. Don't even think about that or Officer Tight Pants is going to undergo some surgery, right here. No, you'd better drop the gun and slide it across the floor to me, real easy."

He motioned with his pistol, and I obeyed.

"Why are you doing this?" I asked. "You can't get away, but you can come out of this alive if you give up now. Release her and drop your gun. I won't let anybody hurt you."

"Oh, I'll only be a minute and then I'm off, so I will get away with it, just like all the others. I've got to get away, don't you see? Mr. Tommy Shea, you've heard of him, will be very impressed when he learns that I got you AND all these other nice officers, too. What a score. I'll become his right hand man, so to speak."

"So, that's it. You're a stooge for Shea."

He poked the knife into Karen again and she screamed, as more blood flowed. "Watch it, Detective. I'm nobody's stooge. Shea doesn't even know me yet, but he will. He sure will."

I looked at Pearson for his weapon, but it was gone. Hoodie didn't have it, though, so it must be around someplace. I had to find it.

"I can see out the front window from here," said Hoodie. It looks like you've got another female officer standing guard. How nice, but she's not as good as Officer Tight Pants."

"I heard a gunshot a minute ago," I said. "What happened?"

"Oh, please, Detective, don't play the fool. You know you had a man out back. I'm afraid he had to take one for the team, don't you know. He won't be any more trouble. Tsk, tsk."

I was silent. My fists clenched and I stared at the floor. Leo.

"Oh, don't be so sad, Detective. Look on the good side. Because of me, you got to see the lovely boobs on this fine young lady. That never would have happened, if not for me. Hah, ha, ha. You know, I was thinking of cutting one off, like a guy did in that Harold Robbins book a few years back. It was a western story and the guy killed an Indian squaw, cut off her tit and made a tobacco pouch out of it. Hah, what an idea. Robbins sure wrote some cool stuff."

"How far do you think you can get? We've got cars coming right now and they'll circle this area. You can't get away on foot or in a car. There'll be helicopters, too, and the State Police has been notified. You're stuck, so why don't you just release her and give up? I can guarantee your safety."

I needed time for the help to arrive, but I also worried about Leo. Maybe he was still alive and needed medical help. I was running out of options.

"Screw you, cop," yelled Hoodie. "You think I've been working this plan just to give up now? That boozeman was just the start. And that college teacher, I was having fun cutting her into her principle parts. I bet that one brought back memories for you. YOU WERE NEVER GOING TO GET

ME. I'M TOO SMART FOR ALL OF YOU. AND TOMMY'S GOING TO LOVE ME. TIME TO SAY GOODNIGHT."

He pushed the knife deeper into Karen and her scream filled the air. I had to rush him. There was no choice. I stood up, staring at Hoodie and I gritted my teeth, awaiting the gunshot as I clenched my fists, about to make my rush. I heard the shot, but felt nothing. Instead, Hoodie's head exploded, as a bullet ripped through it from behind. He fell forward, still holding Karen close to him, the knife still in his hand, the blade partially in her stomach. She went unconscious.

I saw a tall man enter from the kitchen and felt enormous relief that my partner was okay.

"Well, ain't this a fix, wop cop? How am I ever going to live this one down, me saving your bacon? I think I'm going to be sick."

It wasn't Leo. It was Tommy Shea.

There was no time for explanations. I put my hand on top of Hoodie's and eased the knife out of Karen, pushing him away and turning her onto her back. I whipped off my jacket and covered her, as much as I could, before taking a handkerchief out of my pocket and pressing it against her wound.

"I'll do that, Contino. I know something about knife wounds. Go help your buddy, Barbado. He took one in the thigh. I used his belt for a tourniquet. Good thing for him this fat guy's a lousy shot."

I backed away, amazed at what I was seeing, Shea helping a cop. I went to the front door and yelled for Officer Heard to come in. "It's all clear."

She ran up to the door, gripping her weapon, pointed down.

"You can stand down, Officer. Call for an ambulance, then help Pearson. I've got to get to Leo out back."

She holstered her gun. "Who's this, sir?" she asked, looking at Shea.

"Later."

I ran through the kitchen and out the open back door into to the yard, where Leo lay on his back, his hands behind his head, as if he was resting. His right foot was propped up on a yard chair, elevating his wounded leg.

"I thought you'd never get here, Detective. What took you so long?"

"You . . . Christ, you took a hell of a time to take five. I figured you for dead."

"Yeah, well Mr. Hoodie can't shoot for shit and, once I went down, I guess he figured he had me. And look who my lifesaver turns out to be. Holy shit!" His face went grim and his tone changed. "How's it inside?"

"Hoodie's dead. Orlando's been stabbed, but I don't think it's deep. Pearson took a knock on the head. He'll be okay. But jeeze, Tommy Shea coming to the rescue. I'm going to need a few stiff belts after this one."

"WE'RE going to need a few, partner. And keep them coming."

Chapter Forty-Four

Shea knew the drill.

He surrendered his weapon to me without a problem. "It's a perfectly legal piece, Detective, and I've got a valid permit to carry. So, now we go to HQ and you get my statement. Well, I'm just a good old citizen, eager to help."

I shook my head as I took his weapon, unloaded it, and put it in my pocket with the bullet clip. This gun saved the lives of me and four other officers.

After the ambulance arrived and attended to my officers and Leo, I was ready to talk to Shea. I wanted to ride to the emergency room with my people, but I had to deal with him. I knew the others were okay, now.

I retrieved my weapon off the floor and found Pearson's tucked in Hoodie's belt behind his back. I left it there.

Shea had taken a seat on the living room sofa, while waiting for the ambulance and the rest of the law enforcement personnel. He was so patient and peaceful, I thought I might be dreaming. I nodded to him that it was time for us to leave.

We got into the back seat of my car after I gave the keys to Officer Heard and we headed back to HQ.

"You've got some explaining to do, Shea. This better be good. What the hell are you doing here?"

"Why, saving your sorry asses, Detective. Never thought I'd live to see the day, but here it is. You got any booze?"

"Come on, what's your connection to Hoodie?"

"Hoodie? Is that what you call him? I guess it'll do."

I wet my lips. "So, you really don't know the guy."

"Nope. But I was going to."

"That's what he said. He admitted you don't know him, but he was planning to make this hit on me and the others as a way of impressing you. He's been killing people on the Cape in ways that bear some resemblance to prior cases of mine. That took some figuring. At first, it looked like we had a serial killer loose. But, eventually we put the pieces together. So, how did you get on his trail?"

Shea sat legs crossed at the knee, his hands folded on his lap, as calm as could be for somebody who just blew another guy's brains out. "He came into Club 77 a short time ago. He paid for play with Ginny. You remember Ginny? Then he sits at the bar talking to Big Ted and sends a round of drinks to my table. He gets up and waves to me as he walks out. I sent my friend to follow him and he got the make and license on his car. So, I was able to find out who he is and where he lives."

I glared at him. His reach always amazed me.

"I read about some stuff he did. It was in the Boston paper, him screaming my name out while he tries to ace some guy. I didn't like it. He was dragging me into stuff I didn't have anything to do with. That can be bad for my reputation, you know. I don't need the extra heat. I decided to give him a call today, but he was driving away from his place as I arrived, so I followed him, to see what he was up to."

"Why did you pick today?"

"Just coincidence. I was getting tired of this creep and wanted to give him a message. So, he thought I was going to like his methods, huh? What an ass. Guess where he was going, Detective."

"No games, Shea. Just fill me in."

"He drove to your department. He parked across the street past the intersection. He watched for your girlie officer to drive away. He must have staked her out before. I followed him to her house and parked up her street a ways, then you guys showed up in all your glory. I got up close on foot. I heard some noise and then he hit Barbado in the leg. Now, I figure, this might be a chance for me to do some civic good while ridding me of a problem, so I decided to help Barbado, then see what you might need inside.

"I figured you'd have backup coming, but time was not in your favor. I worked my way inside and saw that things were about to go south for you. You're a tough egg, Detective, I'll give you that, but I don't know if you could survive another gut shot. Of course, your backup soldiers would have blown the guy to smithereens later, but I decided to save them the expense. I didn't want a creep like that to be the one who aces you."

"Gee, Shea, I didn't think you cared."

"I don't, wop cop, but I had to solve my problem, too."

"So why didn't you let him shoot me and then you get him?"

"Naw, it'd be too hard to explain if I was the last man standing in there. Who'd believe me? Hell, even you deserve better than getting it from a creep like him."

It was as strange a scenario as I could ever have imagined. We figured out what Hoodie was up to and were prepared to take him, but he kept us on the defensive and it took a lucky break in the form of a hardened criminal helping us out. Sometimes, you just don't know where your luck will come from, if it comes at all.

About the Author

Steve Marini holds a Master's degree in Educational Technology from Boston University and a B.A. in Business Administration from New England College and has spent over thirty years in the Education/Training field, including posts in higher education and the federal government.

Although he describes himself as a "card carrying New Englander," he lived for twenty-six years in Maryland while pursuing a career spanning four federal agencies. His background has enabled him to serve as a project manager at the National Security Agency, the Environmental Protection Agency, the National Fire Academy and the Centers for Medicare and Medicaid Services, where he worked with teams of experts in various fields to develop state-of-the-art training for both classrooms and distance learning technologies.

A "Baby Boomer," Steve has taken up fiction writing as he moved into his career final frontier. Married for thirty-six years, a father of three and a grandfather, Steve and his wife Louise own a home on Cape Cod that will serve as his private writer's colony for the years ahead.

WEBSITE: www.stevenmarini.com
BLOG: http://babyboomerspm.blogspot.com/
FACEBOOK: http://www.facebook.com/StevenPMarini
TWITTER: https://twitter.com/StevenPMarini